THE GUN MASTER

They lived in the shadow of a fear that grew by the hour, dreading the moment when their world would be destroyed by a torrent of looting and murder. And when that day finally dawned, the folk of Peppersville knew they would be standing alone against the notorious Drayton Gang. There was not a gun in town that could match the likes of the hard-bitten, hate-spitting raiders. But now it looked as if change was on the way with the arrival of the new schoolteacher, the mysterious McCreedy . . .

LUTHER CHANCE

THE GUN MASTER

Complete and Unabridged

LINFORD
Leicester

First published in Great Britain in 2004 by
Robert Hale Limited
London

First Linford Edition
published 2005
by arrangement with
Robert Hale Limited
London

The moral right of the author
has been asserted

British Library CIP Data

Chance, Luther
    The gun master.—Large print ed.—
Linford western library
1. Western stories
2. Large type books
I. Title
823.9'14 [F]

ISBN 1–84395–914–3

Published by
F. A. Thorpe (Publishing)
Anstey, Leicestershire

Set by Words & Graphics Ltd.
Anstey, Leicestershire
Printed and bound in Great Britain by
T. J. International Ltd., Padstow, Cornwall

This book is printed on acid-free paper

This one is for J with fond regard

1

By the high summer of that year the folk of Peppersville could only wait, wondering if the next shadow to darken the street would be the one they lived in dread of ever seeing.

'Just ain't no sayin' to it, is there?' storekeeper Byron Byam had pronounced, and not for the first time. 'They might hit town tomorrow, might be next week, next month. Who's to know? Only certainty we got is that they ain't goin' to ride round us. And that's for fact. Can't say other. T'ain't in their nature, or whatever passes for minds in their animal heads. I ain't never heard, not once, of them Drayton scum passin' up a pickin' that happens across their trail. And that's for another fact. And don't nobody argue they ain't headin' this way. 'Course they are. Damnit, I can darned near smell 'em!'

He was not alone in his belief. Saloon owner Clyde Harte was in no doubt of the prospect facing them. 'Way I see it,' he had been quick to declare on news of the impending danger, 'we've just got to be prepared. Ain't no point in sittin' around discussin' it. We need to be ready, get organized, have some sort of plan.'

'And what would that be, Mr Harte?' undertaker Ephraim Judd had asked, peering dolefully over his polished pince-nez. 'You care to outline your thinkin', sir?'

'Well, I ain't rightly got to the detail, you understand. I mean, that takes time and studyin' through. Gotta think carefully. Mebbe we should elect a committee, form a council or somethin'.'

But talk of committees and councils had found little favour among the generally independent folk of Peppersville. They were not of an inclination to put themselves so readily on what one described as a 'war footing'.

'After all, what have we really got to go on?' a town man had asked, drawing expansively on a large cigar. 'Well, I'll tell you. We got only the word of a travellin' purveyor of two-bit medicines that the Draytons are on the rampage north of the Big Moon mountains and reckoned to be headin' south — which, I agree, would put us right in their path if they hold to the main trail. *If* they do. But who's to say they will, save the medicine man? It's only his word.'

'And it seemed sound enough to me,' Byam had persisted. 'Fella weren't lyin'. Why should he? Told his story straight up, didn't he? You all heard him. Said he'd seen first-hand up Leverton way how Frank Drayton had led his boys and his brothers on an all-time burnin', lootin', rapin' raid through the town 'til there weren't nothin' of note and darned near nobody standin'. Saw it all, he said. Beginnin' to end. Worst he'd ever seen.'

Byam had nodded knowingly as he

took a hold of the lapels of his tailored frock coat.

'Well, I sure heard the fella tell it just like that,' the doleful undertaker had agreed, shifting his pince-nez into place. 'And he weren't lyin' none. I can sniff out a tall tale when I hear it, and this was for genuine. Had to be when he told what he'd heard Frank declare. This was only a beginnin', he'd said, just a start. Promised as how he'd scorch and pillage the territory to a stinkin' cinder in retribution for the shootin' of his younger brother, Lloyd. Said just that — a stinkin' cinder, the whole territory.' The pince-nez had slipped on a sudden surge of sweat. 'Plain enough to my ears.'

'Mine too,' a tobacco-chewing man had offered in support. 'And I ain't in no doubt as to precisely where that places us: we're plumb at the centre of the territory. No question of it. Looked it up on the map hangin' in Sheriff Palmer's office.'

The cigar-smoking man had coughed

and spluttered on an intake of smoke. 'We all know where we are, damn it! Don't need no map to tell us that. All I'm sayin' — '

This had been the all-too-familiar cue for the Sheriff to heave his tall, heavily-built frame to its full height and, waiting a moment for the gathering in the saloon bar of the Broken Nugget to fall silent, cast a long thoughtful gaze over the assembly.

'Said it before, but I'll say it again, anyhow,' he began with the gaze relaxed and settled. 'We watch. We wait. We don't get to exhaustin' ourselves with panic talk. But that don't mean to say we do nothin'.'

'So what are we doin', Sheriff?' a grey-faced man had called.

'Told you that before, but, seein' as how I read how you're all feelin', I'll tell you again: I've got deputies on a round-the-clock watch on the main trail into town, and I've got them keepin' a regular eye on the lesser tracks and trails through the mountains. There ain't nobody, and I mean nobody, headin' for Peppersville that I don't know about long before he gets here, day or night, rain or shine. And I shan't be lettin' up on that, leastways not 'til I know a deal more about the Drayton gang's intentions.'

'Yeah, what about them Draytons?' the grey-faced man had asked. 'Is there anybody who's got any idea what they're plannin'? Damn it, they can't treat Leverton like they did and get away with it. Somebody's got to bring 'em to book.'

'And somebody will, don't you fret on that,' the Sheriff had assured. 'Meantime, I'm doin' all I can to try to keep up with the gang's movements. At this precise moment, they seem to have gone to ground. They're lyin' low, keepin' quiet, which is a silence that bothers me some.'

'Me too,' had come the voice from behind the cigar smoke.

'Say that again,' another voice had added, only to be joined, as it usually was, by a buzz of murmuring.

It was at this point that a quick glance from the Sheriff would bring Doc Walker from the shadows to his side. 'Stayin' vigilant, keepin' your eyes open and reportin' anythin' unusual is what you've all got to do,' the Sheriff went on. 'And Doc here's got a word to say on that.'

'Don't have to tell you good folk that no two days are the same,' Doc had begun. 'Seems that way sometimes, I know, but it's often the little things that count: the new face around town that passes unnoticed; the hitched mount you ain't seen before; some innocent traveller's comment . . . Anyone might give us just the time we need to be ready for the Draytons, because, believe me, them scum are just as capable of wriggling into town like soft-bellied snakes, as they are of hellraisin' down the trail. So, like the sheriff says, watch and wait. We're goin' to be fightin' here for our town as well as our lives.'

'And Amen to that,' Preacher Peabody had murmured after clearing his throat carefully but deliberately. 'And Doc might have added that we are also defending our increasingly hopeful future, specially in the light of the arrival any day now of Peppersville's first full-time teacher, Mr McCreedy. Comes to us highly recommended and fully qualified from back East. Yessir, only the best for the young of Peppersville!'

But Preacher Peabody's words had passed largely unheard and few, if any it seemed, paid much attention when the teacher finally rode into town two days later.

2

'I seen him. Lean, rangy fella. Don't say a deal, I hear. Taken a room with Preacher Peabody 'til they get to fixin' up the schoolhouse. Don't look much of a teacher type to me, but that ain't surprisin', seein' as how I never went to school!'

Sheriff Palmer grunted to himself, glanced quickly at his early morning visitors and came wearily to his feet from behind his desk. 'Frankly, I ain't got the time for botherin' with teachers right now. We've got other problems.'

He crossed to the map hanging on the wall of his office and stabbed a finger into a shadowed area of mountains. 'There. One of 'em's been seen at Sandy Pass. About noon yesterday. My deputy reckons it was Frank Drayton's brother, Charlie.'

The sheriff held his finger in position

for a moment, his stare tight on the spot, then grunted again and turned back to his visitors.

'And what do you glean from that?' asked Byron Byam, squinting into the shadowed area on the map.

'Assumin' the sightin' to be authentic, of course,' added the undertaker, adjusting his pince-nez.

'I ain't no reason to doubt what my deputy seen,' said Palmer, crossing to his desk. 'As to what I figure, we got two possibilities: one, the Draytons and the rest of the gang cleared Leverton and headed straight for some hideout in the Big Moon range. Charlie was mebbe just keepin' watch. Or two: the main body of the gang was movin' through the range, headin' God-knows where, and Charlie was scoutin' out the trail.'

'You mean they might be skirtin' round us?' said Byam through the glimmer of a half-smile.

Ephraim Judd locked his hands in a fierce grip behind him. 'More likely figurin' on how to avoid the main trail into here,' he pecked out disdainfully, his shoulders hunching.

Sheriff Palmer sighed. 'Got to admit you're probably right, Ephraim. Mebbe that's precisely what Charlie was doin'.'

'But if that's the case, if what you say is true, then they could be here anytime,' groaned Byam, beginning to sweat. 'Today . . . Tonight! Damn it, we should be doin' somethin', f'crissake.'

'Hold on there,' said Palmer, raising an arm. 'We've been through all that. Talked ourselves into a corner over what might or might not be done. Fact is, as far as this particular sightin' is concerned, we've now got an area we can pinpoint and concentrate on. I've got two men watchin' Sandy Pass right now. If Drayton and his gang are figurin' on headin' for Peppersville from that direction, we're goin' to know about it the minute they raise dust.'

'Glad to hear it,' murmured Byam, swallowing deeply. 'We're goin' to need all the warnin' we can get, specially if — '

'Two strangers ridin' in now,' said Judd peering through the dusty window overlooking the street. 'Where the devil did they spring from?'

'Hell,' mouthed Palmer, coming to the undertaker's side, Byam already at his shoulder.

'Don't look none too savoury to me,' muttered the storekeeper, twitching under the sting of his sweat. 'You seen 'em before, Sheriff?'

'Never, and I ain't for havin' 'em around long enough to get familiar. Leave this to me.'

In the next minute Sheriff Palmer had strapped on his gunbelt and headed into the street.

*   *   *

Sheri Ward stretched, yawned, ran her fingers down her face and into her neck, and grimaced at the foul taste in her mouth.

Some night, she thought, blinking on the shimmer of sunlight in the street below her. Business through the Broken Nugget had been brisker than ever. She grimaced again and tossed her loose hair into her neck. So much for the menfolk of Peppersville feeling under threat. Or maybe they had been drowning their sorrows.

She shrugged. Who cared? Time might be coming when there would be no Broken Nugget, let alone any business. Make a dollar while it lay on the table was her philosophy, leastways for now until the day dawned when she had all the dollars she needed and could realize her dreams. Meantime, there was this day and whatever it might deliver.

She had half turned from the window when she saw the riders.

Sheri stepped back instinctively to the shadows of her room, lifting herself on tiptoes to peer into the street again, the sounds of the scuff of hoofs, creak of leather and jangle of tack moving closer.

Morgan Reights and Nate Jones, she thought on a tingling shiver, guns for hire whenever and wherever the price was right. She had crossed them some years back during her days through Nevada territory, days now best forgotten. She stifled another shiver, tossed her hair again and edged a foot closer to the window.

No mistaking them, she grimaced, watching their faces as the riders made their slow way down the street. Reights with that same, permanently fixed expression of cynicism etched into his tanned, weathered skin. Jones, an altogether paler, thinner man who still looked as if he had squirmed from beneath a wet stone.

But what were they doing in Peppersville? What dollars-for-fast-guns deal had lured them here, and was it coincidental that they were arriving in the wake of the pillage at Leverton and the Drayton gang's rumoured threat?

She watched anxiously as the gun-slingers hitched their mounts and stepped to the boardwalk fronting the Broken Nugget.

* * *

'Mite early for us to be openin' the bar, fellas, but I got some fine hot coffee brewin' back there.' Clyde Harte's smile flitted across his lips like a brief break in grey clouds as he struggled into his waistcoat on his way through the batwings to greet the riders. 'Breakfast along of it if you've a mind,' he added thinly.

The gunslingers stood their ground on the boardwalk, their bodies unmoving, hands easy at their sides, eyes fixed and steady on the saloon-keeper.

'Rooms too if you boys are plannin' on stayin',' Harte flustered on, his fingers fumbling with the buttons of his waistcoat. 'Didn't catch your names there.'

'Didn't give none,' grunted Reights,

sidling his weight to one hip.

Jones hawked and spat back into the street. 'Depends,' he muttered. 'Mebbe we'll stay awhiles. Mebbe we won't.' He spat again then tightened his gaze on Harte's flushed face. 'Either way, we ain't much for coffee.'

'Sure, sure,' grinned Harte, gesturing to the 'wings. 'I'll open the bar m'self. Right now. Drinks on the house.' He glanced over the men's shoulders to the shadowed street, his eyes working frantically for a glimpse, he hoped, of Sheriff Palmer. 'Always good to see new faces around town. You bet. You boys travelled far? Livery's far end of town.' He pushed open a 'wing. Old Stoney — he's our blacksmith — does a fine job. Comes recommended.'

The men had reached the 'wings when the voice rang out at their backs.

'Hold it right there, fellas. Not another step.'

The sheriff strode purposefully down the middle of the street, his boots scuffing rhythmically through the dirt, a soft shimmer of dust lifting in his wake, his stare unblinking on the saloon.

Morgan Reights turned slowly, a nerve twitching in his cheek. Jones paused a moment, his gun hand dropping instinctively to within a whisper of his holstered Colt, then eased his body round as if oozing it through mud.

'Sheriff,' called Harte, releasing the batwing. 'We've got some early visitors.'

'So I see,' quipped Palmer, striding on.

3

'Goin' to have to ask you to hand over your sidearms, boys,' said Palmer, stepping from the street to the boardwalk at the Broken Nugget. 'Town rules. No guns save those worn by officers of the law — them bein' myself and my deputies.'

'Since when?' sneered Reights, one eye hooded in its concentration on the sheriff's face.

Palmer hesitated, his gaze flattening like the threat of bad weather. 'Since I decided,' he answered, the gaze unmoving.

Nate Jones was tempted to spit, but thought better of it. 'You got some personal thing about guns, or us in particular?' he asked, lounging his weight.

'Nothin' personal,' said Palmer. 'Just town rules.'

'That's right,' flustered Harte, fidgeting with his waistcoat. 'Town rules, like the sheriff here says. No guns and no exceptions.'

'All right, Clyde, leave this to me.' Palmer flicked his gaze irritably to the saloon-keeper. 'Just hand over your guns, fellas, and collect 'em from my office when you pull out.' He paused. 'I take it you're only passin' through?'

'We please ourselves,' growled Reights. 'Fact is we might be stayin' awhiles. We got business here.'

'What sort of business?' asked Palmer carefully.

'Well, now,' grinned Jones, 'that's for us to be knowin', ain't it? T'ain't really of no concern to you. It's kinda personal.'

'Right now everythin' in this town concerns me, especially when it comes to the business of strangers.'

'And that's puttin' it mildly,' nodded Harte, disregarding the sheriff. 'You fellas may not have heard, but there's been real trouble out Leverton way.'

19

'All right, Clyde,' snapped Palmer to no avail as Harte blustered on.

'Too right there was. Whole town shot up by the Drayton gang. You heard of the Draytons? Well, I'll tell you somethin' now: if you ain't heard of the Draytons, you're sure as hell goin' to if you hang about here long enough. Yessir. Ain't that so, Sheriff?'

Palmer seethed quietly, but stayed silent.

'There's a lot of talk — and it ain't all rumour neither — that them murderin' scum — ' began Harte again.

'Enough, Clyde!' flared Palmer. 'All we're interested in here is these fellas' guns. Right now.'

Jones finally spat into the street as he hooked his thumbs into his belt.

Reights cracked his knuckles and levelled a deep stare into Palmer's face.

Harte swallowed, backed to the batwings and began to sweat.

'I said right now,' repeated Palmer, aware out of the corner of his eye of figures beginning to gather silently in the street: Byron Byam, Doc Walker, Ephraim Judd, his undertaker's eyes narrowed on the staring gunslingers as if sizing them for their coffins, Old Stoney, a handful of youngsters and anxious mothers. 'You town folk keep your distance,' he called without shifting his concentration from the men facing him.

'Well, mebbe we can find some compromise here,' flustered Harte, licking his lips. 'Hell, t'ain't beyond us to find some middle ground, is it? I mean — '

'Will you just keep out of this, Clyde?' snapped Palmer again. 'Now,' he quipped, 'am I gettin' them guns, or do I have to take 'em from you?'

'You can sure as hell try, Sheriff,' grinned Jones. 'I, for one, ain't stoppin' yuh. What you reckon, Morgan?'

Reights flexed his fingers. 'I say we let the sheriff have our guns. One at a time. You first.'

Palmer had already stiffened, drawn his Colt in a flourish of flesh to leather when Nate Jones's shot from the hip spun the weapon from his grip to send it clattering across the boardwalk.

'Sonofabitch!' mouthed the sheriff, sucking at a trickle of blood on his hand.

Harte blinked and grabbed the batwings. A woman screamed. The street gathering backed towards the shadows.

'You want I should finish this, Nate?' smiled Reights. 'Won't take a minute, then we can go enjoy that drink we've been promised.'

'Sure,' sneered Jones, 'you go right ahead. Pesterin' lawmen are as bad as pesky flies — ain't they just? So let's put an end to this specimen's buzzin', shall we?'

Palmer had stepped back, gripping his wounded hand, his eyes darker now with the reality of what was about to happen. Harte's mouth dropped open. Sheri Ward gasped from somewhere deep within the shadowy bar.

The woman screamed again.

Byam took a step forward, only to be restrained by the undertaker. 'Don't mess,' urged Judd, laying a hand on the storekeeper's arm.

Doc Walker was easing through the townsfolk to the boardwalk, his gaze held as if in a trance on Reights' slow levelling of his gun on the sheriff, when two shots rang out and two men fell dead with barely a grunt or a groan between them.

Nobody made a sound until the woman who had screamed shuddered into sobs.

★ ★ ★

'So whose rifle is it? How come you, McCreedy, got your hands on it? And just where in the name of charity did a book-readin', pen-pushin' school teacher from back east get to learnin' to shoot like that?' Sheriff Palmer winced as he cradled his bandaged hand.

Byron Byam consulted his timepiece with the air of a man about to pronounce judgement. 'Them varmints survived Peppersville for just fifty-seven minutes. I timed it.'

Ephraim Judd wrote carefully across a page of his black leather notebook. 'That has been duly noted, Mr Byam.'

Preacher Peabody coughed politely behind his hand and adjusted the folds of his coat. 'I admit to ownership of the rifle, Sheriff. I cannot deny it. But it was held purely as a means of defence come the day when . . . well, never mind. It has never been fired, leastways not since coming into my possession, until today. And if I am truthful to my conscience, and surely that of my flock here in Peppersville, I am glad, nay, relieved, that it has been done so by one who very obviously knew how to use it.' He smiled quietly and nodded to McCreedy.

'Amen to that,' said Doc Walker, reaching across the bar to pour the sheriff another drink.

'You bet,' agreed Harte. 'I ain't never seen nobody — not hereabouts anyhow

— handle a gun, any gun, like you did, Mr McCreedy. So where did you acquire the know-how?'

'Who taught the teacher?' quipped Byam, pocketing his timepiece.

The gathering in the still shadowy saloon where a handful of the more courageous and curious lingered at the batwings and windows, fell silent, their gazes settled on the tall, slimly built man in the dark suit and hat standing apart at the far end of the bar, his expression relaxed but firm, his eyes watchful.

'Here and there,' murmured McCreedy, his hands flat on the bar. 'It sometimes pays.'

'Well, it sure as hell paid today,' grinned Harte. 'Say that again, eh, folks?' He looked for support from the gathering. 'Yessir.'

'Mr McCreedy's business is his own affair,' said Doc. 'T'ain't for us to be probin' — just grateful.' Doc nodded to the calls of 'Hear, hear', then added: 'What we need to be askin' here is, who them fellas were, where'd they come from, and what brought them to Peppersville?'

'Doc's right,' called a man from the 'wings. 'What were they doin' here?'

'Weren't in town for the scenery,' said another.

'Nor for their health, or ours come to that,' gestured a third. 'Damnit, they'd have shot the sheriff through like a dog if it hadn't been for McCreedy here.'

The men began to talk animatedly among themselves, some of them spilling through the 'wings into the bar.

'Well, I'm for figurin' it all to do with that Drayton gang,' came a louder voice. 'Them scum sure looked as if they'd be the types to ride with the likes of Frank Drayton. One look was enough for me.'

'One smell did it for me!' clipped a pipe-sucking old-timer.

'Mebbe, mebbe,' said the sheriff, stepping from the bar. 'But if they were plannin' on teamin' up in some way with the Draytons, we did ourselves one big favour — or Mr McCreedy did.'

'Sure we did,' said Byam, 'and that's no bad thing — 'ceptin' for the reaction we're goin' to get from the rats when the gunslingers don't show up, or Frank and Charlie Drayton get to hear of what happened here this mornin'.'

The undertaker murmured and nodded. The gathering fell silent again.

'Morgan Reights and Nate Jones. Crossed them way back out Nevada territory,' announced Sheri Ward across the silence as she reached the foot of the stairs from the balcony above the bar. 'Guns for hire to the highest price. Anybody, anywhere, anytime. They weren't fussy. Shoot to kill, quick and fast. No questions asked.' She stood perfectly still and turned a long, penetrating gaze over the faces watching her, finally bringing it to rest on McCreedy. 'And you've sure as the devil's touch opened a nest of rattlers with the killing of them. Mark my words.'

4

Preacher Peabody raised his eyes to the heavens, murmured a silent prayer and slid silently into the room, closing the door softly behind him. He waited a moment, gathering his breath, swallowing, adjusting his eyes to the gloom before sighing and stepping carefully to the chest of drawers at the draped window.

This was against all his principles. To offer a fellow man shelter beneath your own roof, was one thing — and generous enough of heart at that — but to then set about a search of it and the man's personal belongings, was another, even in the excuse of it being justified.

Ah, but was it, he wondered, closing his eyes?

McCreedy had shown himself to be extremely resourceful, not to say fearless, in the shooting of the two gunmen. That had been a wholly justifiable act of legitimate defence against overwhelming odds.

But for it then to be assumed that there was more to the man than met the eye and 'we should be knowin',' as Sheriff Palmer had put it, was not so easily excused or explained.

Just because a man could handle a gun and shoot fast and accurate did not make him a target of suspicion with hidden depths and a dark past, did it? Or did it?

The preacher murmured again and opened his eyes on the sight of his hands already poised to open the top drawer of the chest . . .

Sheriff Palmer, Doc Walker and the others had been positively insistent once McCreedy had left the bar of the Broken Nugget and wandered away to the street.

'No arguin' it,' Palmer had said, 'we've gotta know more about the fella. Damn it, he saved my life!'

'But that ain't the real nub of it, is it?' Byron Byam had urged. 'Fact is, we can't have a fella of the likes of McCreedy around at this time, with the threat of the Draytons breathin' down our necks, and *not* take account of him, can we? Hell, a gun like his is goin' to be worth its weight in gold when it comes to the crunch.'

'Now hold on there,' Doc had countered, 'McCreedy is here as a teacher. We're goin' to be payin' him for his knowledge and ability to teach our young 'uns, not for his skill with a gun.'

'Goin' to get involved anyhow, ain't he?' Harte had said, leaning on the bar. 'Can't stay in Peppersville and not face what we reckon is comin', can he?'

'Get to teachin' the Draytons a lesson or two, eh?' the old-timer had croaked.

'But we don't know McCreedy will want to fight, do we?' Doc had persisted. 'We only know he's a teacher.'

'And a whole sight somethin' else,'

the sheriff had added. 'And there's only one man in a position to mebbe find the answers.'

Those still gathered in the bar had fallen silent again when Palmer finally turned slowly, carefully to face the preacher. 'Fella's roomin' with you, Mr Peabody. Holed up with his belongin's in your place. Now, I ain't for askin' you to do nothin' unlawful; simply that you sorta take a glance through his possessions just lookin' — only lookin', mark you — for anythin' that might tell us more about who he is. And if that pricks your conscience in any way, think of it as a service to our community . . . '

The drawer slid open like a soft breath released.

⋆ ⋆ ⋆

Preacher Peabody's fingers worked quickly through the contents of the drawer, his mind reeling with confused thoughts, eyes dancing in his head, the sudden heat of the room clamouring round him. Change of shirts, longjohns, clean socks, spare belt — he rifled through the items, turning them against their folds, then turning them back again, thinking hurriedly of their position as he had found them. Nothing he would not have expected. Hardly surprising. What, in any case, was he looking for?

He closed the drawer and opened the next.

His fingers fell across a neatly scored and folded parchment package. He eased it apart without actually lifting it from the drawer and tilted his head to peer closer. A map of the area, he decided, licking at a hot trickle of sweat into his lips. Nothing surprising or incriminating about that. A new arrival in Peppersville planning on staying would naturally want a map.

He was about to move on when he noticed a smaller, thinner sheet of paper tucked within the main fold.

He hesitated. Should he remove it?

Read it? It might be personal. But something 'personal' was precisely what he was looking for, he reminded himself. He licked at the sweat again, blinked and on a silent grimace of concentration slid the sheet from the fold.

A telegraph communication, dated some weeks back, timed at noon from North Rocks to Winston. It read: *Party moving South main trail* and was signed *M.S.*

Preacher Peabody continued to study the text for some moments, his lips moving soundlessly over the brief message. Party, he pondered; who or what was the Party and who was M.S.? McCreedy had said he had reached town from the east. Winston was an eastern town situated plumb on the main trail into Peppersville.

So, mused Peabody, intrigued now by the emerging possibilities, the sender of the wire, M.S., had either learned or seen something in the town of North Rocks concerning the Party he had reckoned important enough to communicate it by telegraph to McCreedy in Winston.

But why . . .

The preacher stiffened at the sound of a movement. Footsteps heading his way. McCreedy had returned.

Peabody folded the sheet of paper, replaced it in the map, closed the drawer and stepped quietly, quickly back to the door.

He listened, his eyes wide and staring. Silence. Where was McCreedy now? The kitchen, living-room? Maybe he was out back taking in the shade of the porch. This was no time for debate. He raised his eyes, offered a silent prayer again and opened the door on the softest turn of the knob.

Preacher Peabody had left the room, collected his hat and was heading in the direction of Sheriff Palmer's office within minutes. He had done all that had been asked of him, probably more if the sheriff or the others could make any sense of the wired message from

North Rocks to Winston.

He had hurried on through the fierce afternoon sun, blissfully unaware of McCreedy slipping into his room and the easy smile on his face when he opened the drawer and noted with no more than a grunt that the parchment map and its contents had been disturbed.

5

Sheriff Palmer stabbed a stiff finger at the map on the wall of his office and grunted like a bad-tempered bear. 'North Rocks,' he growled. 'Who in their right mind would rate North Rocks? What's North Rocks got that ain't ten-for-a-dollar any place else? Tell me that.'

'Someone rated it,' said Doc Walker, mopping the sweat from his hatband.

'Somebody with the initials M.S.,' added Byron Byam, gripping the lapels of his coat. 'Initials which don't mean a thing to me or anybody else hereabouts, I'll wager. And who in tarnation is the Party?'

Ephraim Judd cleared his throat and adjusted his pince-nez. 'I got a theory about that,' he murmured. 'Been givin' it some careful thought.'

'So let's hear it,' urged the sheriff,

turning from the map.

The undertaker shifted the pince-nez again and peered owl-like over the polished rims. 'The Party, I suggest, refers to a person or persons. Thus, the telegraph message as related to us by Preacher Peabody here would translate as meanin' that a person or persons known to both M.S. and McCreedy had ridden out, or was plannin' to ride out of North Rocks headin' south — which, if you then examine the map, might lead you to my next theory.'

'How many theories you got, f'crissake?' mocked Byam as he crossed with the others to face the map.

The preacher, Doc Walker, the storekeeper and Sheriff Palmer gazed at the map as if expecting it to reveal some hidden secret.

'Here,' said Judd, tracing the main trail from the north. His finger moved slowly, deliberately like the crawl of a determined crab. 'The trail passes through Long Bone, Jamesville, Langton and Mud Creek, not one of them more than a two-bits collection of shacks and rundown booze parlours. The only place of note for fifty miles or more is' — he tapped the finger dramatically — 'Leverton.'

The faces gazing at the map stayed silent and blank for a full minute, the eyes fixed and unblinking.

'Which might mean — ' began Doc carefully.

'Which *does* mean, most certainly in my book,' continued Judd, 'that the likely Party leavin' North Rocks was the Drayton gang.'

'But that's only surmisin', and you can't be sure,' said Byam.

'Perhaps we're becoming obsessed with the Draytons,' muttered the preacher, clasping his hands in front of him.

'Timin' fits,' said the sheriff, turning away to his desk. 'We know when the wire was sent from North Rocks, and we know roughly when the Draytons spat their hell-fire through Leverton. Put the two together, and it fits darned near perfect.'

'Which then leaves us with the sender of the wire — the mysterious M.S.,' pondered Doc.

'Mebbe not so big a mystery,' said Judd.

'Don't tell me, you've got another theory!' quipped Byam.

'Not so much a theory as simple deduction, Mr Byam.' The undertaker positioned his pince-nez with authority. 'M.S., we can safely assume, is a close friend of our new sharp-shootin' teacher, Mr McCreedy. No difficulty there. As to precisely who or what he is, we can have no idea. He is both faceless and nameless. But if we believe the Party to be the Drayton gang, we also know that M.S. and McCreedy have a close interest in both of them and their whereabouts.' He paused. 'Question is: we know precisely where McCreedy is, but where, gentlemen, is M.S.? Did he leave North Rocks and follow the trail south? Did he reach Leverton? Did he *survive* Leverton? And what about the scumbags who died here only hours ago?'

The group gathered in the sheriff's office swung round as one as the door burst open and a dust-caked, sweat-soaked deputy tumbled into the room.

'Riders out Sandy Pass comin' in fast,' he blurted, swallowing rapidly. 'Three, mebbe more. I'd figure for 'em bein' here in under the hour.'

'Hell,' cursed Palmer. 'Drayton's men?'

'Too far away to tell,' gasped the deputy, 'but they're beatin' the dirt like there was no tomorrow.'

'Comin' in search of them gunslingers we're about to bury,' groaned Byam, his pallor turning a sickly grey. 'Sheri was right, we've opened a nest of rattlers. Best thing we can do — '

'Is cut the talk and get busy,' ordered Palmer, wincing at the sudden throb in his bandaged hand. 'Open that gun case there and load me a Winchester.'

Preacher Peabody raised his eyes in

another silent prayer. The undertaker's pince-nez began to mist over behind a beading of sweat. Doc Walker sighed as he loaded the rifle.

'Where's that teacher fella?' murmured Byam as the sheriff hurried to the street.

★   ★   ★

Sheri Ward waited in the shadows of the balcony above the Broken Nugget's bar and watched the activity below her. The saloon was filling fast with town men, young and old, all talking at once, gesturing, pointing, clamouring for drinks in one moment, leaving them half drunk in the next.

'So what we goin' to do?' called a man at the batwings. 'We got a plan?'

'Stand firm and shoot it out,' called the old-timer. 'Don't let the rats draw breath.'

'Mebbe we should block the street. Keep the scum out,' shouted a man at the back of the bar.

'He's right,' agreed another. 'We've got to look to the women and young 'uns. If we keep these fellas out now, the Drayton gang will mebbe think twice about hittin' us.'

'How many are on their way?'

'I heard talk of three.'

'I heard six.'

'Fella here says a dozen. Could be more.'

The men fell to talking and calling among themselves.

'Damnit, if there's only a handful of 'em, what they comin' for anyhow?' asked a youth above the babble.

'Obvious, ain't it?' said the old-timer, helping himself to a measure of whiskey from the nearest bottle. 'It's them fellas the school teacher took out — Reights and Jones. This is where they were due to meet up with the Drayton boys. Somebody's ridin' in to meet 'em.' The old-timer tittered and looked round for another unattended bottle.

'That ain't so funny,' quipped the man at the batwings. 'What you figurin' for bein' their mood when they find out what happened? You thought of that? Wager you ain't.'

There was a deeper murmur of agreement.

'I'll tell you what they'll be reckonin',' chimed a lean, blinking fellow at the bar. 'They'll be reckonin' on revenge, that's what. Revenge. And how in tarnation we goin' to deal with that? We ain't goin' to stand a chance once the news gets back to the Draytons and they bring the whole darned shebang of the gang down on our heads. It'll be a massacre. Every last man, woman — '

A single, ear-splitting gunshot rang out from the boardwalk.

'Any more talk like that and I'll be the one doin' the shootin', so help me God I will!'

Sheriff Palmer held the rifle high, the barrel pointing to the cloudless sky, a wisp of smoke drifting lazily on the whisper of a breeze. He took the few steps to the batwings, prodded them open and stared defiantly round the assembly.

'Do I make myself clear?' he barked, his glare darkening. 'Talk of massacre won't get us nowhere. There'll be no more of it.'

'Easy to say, Sheriff,' mused the old-timer. 'Tain't so simple when you get to reckonin' it through.'

'And sittin' around here full of black talk ain't helpin' neither,' said Doc, coming to the sheriff's side. 'Reactin' out of blind anger is the worst thing we can do.'

'Doc's right,' agreed Palmer, the rifle easy in his grip, his bandaged hand flat across his waist. He rested the tip of the barrel on a table, his eyes moving slowly over the watching faces, probing the drift of smoke haze. He waited until the gathering was silent before continuing. 'We're all livin' under the cloud of what we assume will be the far from welcome arrival of the Drayton gang. There ain't no arguin' to that. The Draytons may or may not ride into town, but my considered judgement now is that they will.'

The men murmured quietly.

Somebody cleared his throat, another moved a bottle.

'How soon?' croaked a barrel-bellied man, mopping his brow.

'No sayin',' clipped Palmer. 'But we might have a whole sight better idea once the riders beatin' hell out of Sandy Pass right now finally hit town.' He paused a moment. 'I want them to ride in unmolested, without bein' challenged. I want them unharmed and here, face-to-face.'

'What in tarnation for?' wheezed the old-timer.

'Because I want to hear all there is to hear about the Drayton mob's plannin', leastways as much as can be gleaned from Charlie Drayton's sidekicks.' Palmer tapped the tip of the rifle on the table. 'So, I want the town cleared and Boot Hill quiet, save for those standin' to me right here. Go home and stay home. That's an order.' He gestured to

Clyde Harte hovering at the foot of the stairs. 'No more drinks. The bar's closed. And get them girls out of sight.'

Harte nodded through a billowing cloud of cigar smoke. The men muttered among themselves and began to leave. The sheriff relaxed the rifle as he slumped wearily into a chair, but Sheri Ward could only shiver in the shadows of the corridor.

She could already feel the chill of what she feared was coming.

6

'So where is he? He left town or somethin'?' Sheriff Palmer spat from the boardwalk to the sun-baked dirt of the street. 'Might have said, damn it.' He shrugged his sticky shoulders. 'There was a whole lot more I wanted to say to Mr McCreedy. Whole lot more I wanted to *know* about him come to that.' He tightened his gaze on the empty street and the silent, shadow-streaked buildings opposite. 'What's your reckonin', Doc? You figure McCreedy's pulled out?'

Doc Walker thrust his hands deep into the pockets of his coat. 'I doubt it,' he said quietly, watching the shimmer of haze where the main trail reached the street. 'He's about, somewhere.'

'Mebbe he's figured for Preacher Peabody searchin' his room,' croaked the storekeeper, swallowing on his dry, dusty throat. 'Or mebbe Ephraim is right and he and that M.S. fella are tied in somehow.' He swallowed again. 'Supposin' he's left to meet him? Supposin' . . . What the hell, what's it matter? He ain't here right now, but we are and we've got company only minutes away.' Byam scrambled his fingers round a bandanna and mopped his brow. 'Where's the lookout posted?'

'Top of the old saddlery,' murmured Palmer.

'He reliable?'

'Sam Denver's got eyes like a hawk. One of my best deputies.'

'I know Sam,' said Doc, his eyes narrowing against the glare. 'He ain't for no messin'. Minute he sees the first dust of them riders, we'll know well enough.' His gaze shifted through a slow scan. 'Town's all quiet. Folk seem to have taken your advice — they're stayin' out of sight.' He glanced quickly at the sheriff. 'So what's your plan?'

'It's like I said, I want to hear as much as the varmints headin' in are ready to spill. If these riders are Drayton's men, and if it is that they're here to meet the gunslingers McCreedy took out, I want to know what the next move's goin' to be.'

'Just like that,' mocked Byam. 'And they're goin' to tell you, aren't they? Oh, sure! More likely put a bullet through your gut!'

'Well, mebbe we'll get to shootin' first,' snapped Palmer. 'Damn it, there's enough of us.'

'And we ain't goin' to be long findin' out,' said Doc, taking a step forward. 'Sam's signallin' now.'

* * *

Preacher Peabody adjusted the set of his broad-brimmed black hat, ran a finger round the sweaty grip of his clerical collar and winced at the thudding beat of the approaching riders.

He squinted through the swirling dust cloud to catch a glimpse of the blurred shapes. One, two, three . . . Five men mounted, low to the necks of their wild-eyed, lathered horses. Dark, silent men, intent on a destination. And they had reached it, thought the preacher seconds later as the thud of hoofs eased to a slither and the dust cloud hung like a shroud across the boardwalk fronting the Broken Nugget.

Preacher Peabody waited a moment, taking time to glance back as if to double check he had locked the neat front door to his clapboard home, then set off at a brisk pace towards the saloon.

He realized, of course, that he was disobeying Sheriff Palmer's explicit orders. 'No need for you to hang about the street, Mr Peabody,' Palmer had said. 'Best get yourself home. Stay there. Stay safe. But if you should happen to see that fella McCreedy . . . '

There had been no sight of the teacher, but no hint either that he had left. So was that a good thing, he had wondered, or was it a sign that McCreedy had opted for keeping a low profile — and out of sight?

How did you stay successfully out of sight in a place like Peppersville, he had pondered briefly? And dismissed the thought in an instant at the first sound of the riders.

He hurried on, hugging the shadows, his gaze concentrated on the saloon, the horses being hitched, the riders dusting the trail dirt from their clothes, one man hawking loudly before spitting. Sheriff Palmer had stepped to the edge of the boardwalk, the Winchester cradled in his arms, Doc Walker and Byron Byam flanking him to left and right.

The five men were grouped at the steps to the batwings, their voices muted at this distance, their stances easy, relaxed, hats pushed clear of sweating brows, arms and hands loose at their sides. Only one man, a lean, snake-faced man, flexed his fingers, nervously spreading and clenching them like restive claws.

The preacher reached the locked and darkened doors of Byam's mercantile, paused, wiped the sweat from his face and slid on again to the next spread of shadow.

The voices grew louder, more distinct.

' . . . so that's the way of it, fellas,' Sheriff Palmer was saying with no more than the flicker of a grin at his lips. 'Law's the law in my town, and no messin'. Somebody, anybody, gets to refusin' to hand over his sidearms and he faces the consequences. Then takes the risk of the outcome. Peppersville law is *the* law 'til I say otherwise. And there ain't no otherwise right now.'

The storekeeper assumed his sternest expression and nodded agreement.

Walker drew himself to his full height as he cleared his throat importantly. 'The men you refer to, Reights and Jones, made that precise mistake,' he said firmly, his gaze steady. 'Pity. But the shootin' was in self-defense and they died quickly and cleanly, I can vouch for that.'

Preacher Peabody closed his eyes, murmured a silent prayer then blinked again on the sunlit street's shimmering glare.

'Best I can offer you is the few belongin's them fellas had with 'em. Not a deal, but you're welcome, assumin', o'course, you're some sorta kin or close friends,' said Palmer, running his good hand over the Winchester.

The five riders stayed silent. Byam swallowed and began to sweat. Doc Walker slid his fingers to the lapels of his coat. The preacher prayed. A tired horse snorted.

'Who shot 'em? Which one of yuh?' asked the snake-faced man, his eyes narrowing to tight slits as he probed the sheriff's face.

'Well — ' began Byam in a fluster of gestures.

'Fella ain't around right now,'

snapped Palmer hurriedly. 'But you can take it from me he's respected hereabouts and ain't no hired gun, if that's what you're thinkin'.'

'Who are you, anyhow?' said Doc, watchful of a black-hatted, weather-tanned rider making his way across the boardwalk to the batwings. 'We ain't heard much by way of introductions.'

'That's right,' nodded Byam enthusiastically, fumbling for his bandanna. 'I ain't heard no names mentioned. You fellas just passin' through?'

Preacher Peabody eased a few steps closer, still hugging the shadows, still with his gaze on the men at the saloon and now, in particular, the fellow who had stepped to the batwings.

The flexing-fingers man spat and then smiled cynically. 'That another of your laws, Sheriff? You want to know everybody's name, date of birth? You want we should give you a family history or somethin'?'

'All I'm askin' — ' But Palmer's protest was dismissed as the man brushed past him to the 'wings, his companions following.

'Now hold on there,' spluttered Byam, only to be pushed back to the wall under the thud of a fist in his chest.

'There ain't no cause for this,' quipped Palmer, ranging the Winchester in his one-handed grip.

The five riders halted, waited, then spun round, drawn Colts tight and levelled in their hands.

'Don't mess with me, lawman,' drawled the snake-faced man, the sweat standing proud on his face, his eyes glinting, gun steady. 'You pull the trigger on that rifle and you and your town men here will be dead in seconds. I do not joke.' He prodded the Colt. 'Now, you drop that rifle and step to the wall, all three of you, hands where we can see 'em. First man, any man, who gets to movin' does so for the last time.'

He turned to the black-hatted man at the batwings. 'Go take a look inside.

Take Cord with you. Grab a girl like Charlie said, and some whiskey. And we want the name of the sonofabitch who shot Morgan and Nate. We'll hang him first.'

7

Sheriff Palmer's nostrils flared in his anger, the sweat of the steadily thickening heat of the day gleaming on his florid face. At his side, Byron Byam's cheeks had sunk to a sickly grey, his eyes dulled in their flat stare. He swallowed noisily in an attempt to find a voice for his words, but stayed silent.

Doc Walker, on the other hand, was in no mood for silence. 'You boys with the Drayton gang?' he asked sharply. 'I guess so. Pretty obvious, ain't it? And you're here to meet up with two new recruits: Reights and Jones. That don't take no figurin' neither.'

The snake-faced man spat into the street.

'So tell me,' continued Doc, 'what was the plan? Were them scumbag gunslingers here to prepare the ground for when the Drayton mob rides in?' He grinned broadly. 'You bet, eh? You bet . . . Well, now, ain't that some burr-in-your-boot situation we've created? I'll say!'

'And don't think you won't be payin' for it, 'cus you sure as hell's fire will, and how,' said snake-face, spinning his Colt through his fingers. 'Charlie Drayton ain't goin' to be one bit happy. And when Charlie ain't happy . . . his retribution is somethin' to behold.'

The gunmen tittered, hawked and spat. A long-haired, dirt-crusted fellow kicked the wall. 'What we waitin' for, f'crissake?' he growled. 'When we gettin' to the action?'

The sheriff winced on the throb in his bandaged hand. 'You ain't reckonin' on gettin' away with this, are you?' he croaked. 'I wouldn't if I were you. Nossir. By the time — '

'Just shut it, lawman,' snapped snake-face, his attention focusing on the bar beyond the batwings and the muted protests and scuffles in its shadows.

'They're takin' Sheri, f'crissake,' groaned Byam through his dry, cracked lips. 'That's her voice. I can hear her.'

Palmer and Doc Walker exchanged hurried glances. Snake-face and his men crowded at the batwings as the noise and struggling heightened.

'Any sight of that teacher fella?' hissed Doc.

'Nothin',' murmured the sheriff. 'If he knows what's good for him he'll be ridin' out fast.'

'What about Clyde?' hissed Doc again. 'Thought he was supposed to be keepin' the girls hidden.'

'Too damned late,' moaned Palmer as Sheri Ward was tumbled through the batwings to the boardwalk in a tangle of limbs, loose hair and torn clothes, a trickle of blood at her mouth, an ugly weal across her bare shoulders darkening to bruising.

* * *

'In the name of the Lord above, what are they doing?' muttered Preacher Peabody from the shadows, his gaze fixed like a beam of light on the Broken Nugget. 'They are surely not — ' He hesitated as Ephraim Judd slid silently to his side.

'An eye for an eye, Mr Peabody,' said the undertaker, peering bird-like over his pince-nez.

'You mean they are goin' to kill Miss Ward in revenge for the deaths of those gunmen, the men McCreedy shot?'

'Not exactly kill her, Mr Peabody,' murmured Judd. 'At least not yet. I imagine they will hold her hostage until they have McCreedy in their hands. And mebbe they'll not kill her even then, though she might be prayin' for it.'

The preacher stifled a deep shudder. 'We must do something. Stop it. What's the sheriff doing?'

'Not a lot he can do right now, leastways not and stay alive. One wrong move and all three of them up there could be dead, not to mention anybody who happens to get in the way. Them fellas are not for reasonin' the rights and wrongs. They shoot fast and first and ask no questions.'

'But we can't allow — ' began the preacher, his voice strengthening and rising.

'Keep your voice down,' urged Judd. 'If they see us, we're dead. You seen McCreedy?'

'No, nothing of him. He wasn't at the house. He's probably left town.'

'His horse is still at the livery. Just spoken to Old Stoney. He says he ain't seen the fella all day.' The undertaker adjusted his pince-nez. 'Don't look good up there, does it?'

Preacher Peabody grimaced at the sting of sweat in his neck. 'Can't hear what they're saying, but the young lady's on her feet — just. Heavens above, she looks sick.'

'Goin' to look a whole lot sicker before them scumbags are through with her,' added Judd darkly.

'Which is precisely why we can't just stand here doing nothing, Mr Judd,' said the preacher, stiffening as he smoothed his coat into place.

'You ain't suggestin' we step out to the street all guns blazin', are you?'

'No, not at all. But can't we raise some of the others? There isn't a soul to be seen. Surely they must know what's going on. Perhaps — '

'Townfolk are doin' what Palmer ordered 'em to do: stayin' indoors and out of sight. Sure we could mebbe raise a dozen men, but it'd be a bloodbath out there. Them's professional guns you're lookin' at, Mr Peabody. Hired killers. Killin's what they do best. Sheriff knows that, and you can wager Doc and Byam ain't overlooked the point.' The undertaker blinked and widened his stare. 'Anyhow, looks as if they're movin'. They're goin' to ride out, takin' Sheri with 'em.'

* * *

'Have I made myself clear, Sheriff?' growled snake-face. 'Produce the man who shot Reights and Jones, deliver him to us at Sandy Pass, or the woman here dies. Couldn't be clearer, could it?' The man holstered his Colt with a flourish. 'You've got twenty-four hours.'

'I'll see you in hell!' croaked Palmer.

'Very likely, but you've still got just twenty-four hours.' Snake-face turned to his men. 'Load the woman on my horse. Take what whiskey you can carry, then we ride, get this two-bits heap of a town out of our sights. But don't fret, boys, we'll be back. You bet we will! And next time we'll watch it burn!'

The gunmen mounted up, reined their snorting horses back to the main trail out of town and had fired a half-dozen loose shots high above their heads when Preacher Peabody stepped briskly into the middle of the street and raised his arms.

'Stop in the name of the Lord Almighty,' he called, the sweat dripping from his face. 'Stop I say!'

'What the hell does the fool think he's doin'?' groaned the sheriff, stepping to the edge of the boardwalk.

'They'll kill him,' croaked Byam.

Doc Walker staggered forward, was tempted for a moment to rescue Palmer's rifle, thought better of it at the shout from the preacher, and could only watch in numbed silence, the blood like ice water through his veins.

'Let the woman go!' screamed the Preacher at the top of his voice. 'Let her go.'

The gunslingers' mounts bucked and pranced, then came on under the momentum of the riders' shouts and yells.

'Stand clear, f'crissake!' called the sheriff, but on deaf ears as the five riders grouped their mounts and charged on.

Preacher Peabody was still standing his ground, still with his arms raised when the hoofs of the first mount struck him and he began to fall. He had only a blurred, fleeting glimpse of the blood-stained face of Sheri Ward before a sudden night closed in and all in the street fell silent.

★ ★ ★

Doc Walker pushed open the batwings to the saloon of the Broken Nugget, stepped inside and surveyed the faces of the town men crowded at the tables, the bar, against the walls, at the foot of the stairs, wherever there was room to plant two feet. He waited a moment for his vision to adjust to the haze of smoke hovering on the dim glow of the night lanterns, then cleared his throat carefully, acknowledged the silent attention afforded him, and spoke his words slowly.

'Preacher Peabody's in a bad way,' he began quietly, 'but he's goin' to live.'

There was a general murmur of relief before the Doc raised a hand for silence. 'But that's where the good news ends,' he continued. He paused, scanning the anxious faces. 'Mr Peabody ain't ever likely to walk again.' The watching faces seemed frozen in time. 'He's sustained one hell of an injury to his spine. The damage, by my reckonin', is permanent. He won't never stand or take another step.'

'Them sons-of-goddamn-bitches,' murmured a man in the shadows, his eyes gleaming in a surge of hatred. 'We'll grind 'em into hell.'

'Killin's goin' to be too good for the rats,' echoed another to the raised voices of agreement.

'Hang 'em real slow!'

'Cripple 'em same as they've done for Preacher Peabody — that's what we should do.'

'Go get the vermin right now, this very night. Hell, if we all ride together . . . '

The voices grew louder. A bottle fell from a table. The smoke haze swam. The handful of bar girls watching from the balcony began to shiver and cluster together like a brood of fledglings.

Saloon proprietor, Clyde Harte,

gazed anxiously over the gathering's fast-changing mood.

Byron Byam stepped quickly to Doc's side. 'We could be headin' for some mob trouble here.' Doc nodded, then caught the eye of Sheriff Palmer.

The butt of the lawman's Winchester thudded on a table top.

'Hold it right there, all of you,' he shouted above the mayhem as a man helped him stand on a chair, his glare over the assembly as tight as a beam of light. 'Know how you feel. Same goes for me, every man, woman and young 'un. But whippin' ourselves into a frenzy now ain't goin' to help nobody — not Preacher Peabody, not Doc there who's got to tend him, not me, not you, and most of all, not Sheri Ward.'

'Sheriff's right there,' called a man on the stairs. 'We should be lookin' to Sheri. Hell, we ain't got long, and what she must be sufferin' don't bear thinkin' to.'

'But we've got long enough if we use the time and our heads to the best advantage,' said Palmer behind another thud of the rifle butt.

'Give the sheriff some space here,' called Harte, adjusting the set of the cigar between his teeth. 'Let's hear what he's proposin' and stop wastin' the time we've got left.'

'That's right,' supported the store-keeper, wiping the sweat from his brow. 'Damnit, ain't that what Preacher Peabody would be urgin' right now?'

'Too right he would,' agreed Ephraim Judd, fixing his pince-nez. 'There's a whole sight too much at stake: Sheri's life, your lives, the survival of the town. We've got to get organized. So listen up there.'

'Floor's yours, Sheriff,' said Doc. 'But make it quick. Time's runnin' out.'

It was as Palmer took a firmer stance on the chair and opened his mouth to speak that the batwings were flung open under the weight of blacksmith and livery owner, Old Stoney, and the assembled heads turned as one to stare at him.

'Thought you should know,' gasped the blacksmith breathing heavily, 'that teacher fella McCreedy's just left town, ridin' fast for Sandy Pass. And he's armed. Twin Colts that look like he was born with 'em.'

8

Nothing had moved through the shadows of the abandoned cabin for nearly an hour; only the eyes, wide and staring had kept watch on the bolted door and dusty, cobweb-coated window.

Sheri Ward listened to her every breath as if to control its sound, its pace, fearful that any shift might bring a face to the window, a hand to the latch of the door. She dared to blink, watch the sudden dance of moonlight through clouds, the spread of thicker shadows, then finally to make the move she had put off since being bundled into the tumbledown ruin.

She edged step by slow step from the corner to the near side of the window. If she could catch a glimpse of anything that might suggest where she had been brought, a sight of the men who had taken her from the Broken Nugget and who they had joined up with, then she might . . .

She hesitated, hugging the wall, at the sound of voices. She frowned, searching her memory for recognition. There was not much doubt, at least one of the men out there in the night was the snake-faced fellow who had seemed to be leading the group of five back at Peppersville. So was this place Sandy Pass, this cabin the one-time hovel of some down-and-out miner panning through the hills for silver? Was it here, as rumour had it, that the Drayton gang had holed up after the sacking of Leverton?

She shuddered against the ache of the bruising across her shoulders, at the memory of snake-face's sidekicks man-handling her from the saloon. She closed her eyes on images of the dusty street and prancing mounts, the shouts, crack of gunfire, and then of Preacher Peabody's raised arms, the fear and anguish on his face as he thudded to the dirt under the surge of hoofs.

Her eyes were open again in an instant at the sound of the voices moving closer. The snake-faced man was still talking, his tone in one moment measured and serious, more light-hearted and animated in the next. The second man spoke only occasionally in clipped grunts.

One of the Drayton boys, wondered Sheri? Were they heading for the cabin? Coming for her?

She tensed, felt a trickle of sweat at her spine and stared into the shadows as if seeking out some deeper, darker place to hide. She shifted again towards the window, her concentration tightening on the little she could make out through the cobwebs draping the dusty pane.

The moonlight picked out the blacker bulks of what might be rocks, boulders, a stack of old timbers, but nothing she could see that moved.

Or was there?

She risked another step, squinting now for what she thought might have been the light catching at something that had glinted for no more than seconds then faded back to the darkness. She squinted again. There was nothing, save the night and the sound of snake-face's voice.

She licked at the sweat on her lip and lifted a shaking hand to brush aside the veil of cobwebs. The view was instantly clearer. Now she could make out the shapes of the rocks, the timbers and the vague outline of a track leading away from the cabin.

She continued to squint, to sweat, then shiver, the voices moving ever closer. Two men on the track, snake-face and a taller man, the words between them lifting and drifting on the night with their slow steps.

' . . . town ain't nothin', Charlie,' snake-face was saying. 'You'll take it faster than you can blink. Just help yourself — stores, whiskey, horses, women — or mebbe you'll fancy torchin' it, eh, like we did Leverton? Burn it or sack it, either way it won't be no trouble. You've got my word on that. Peppersville ain't nothin' but dust and dirt.'

The sweat broke freely on Sheri Ward's brow as she eased a step back from the window, the voices still lifting and drifting.

'Meantime,' grunted the taller man snake-face had called Charlie, 'we've still got to settle with a gunman back there. Losin' Morgan and Nate is somethin' I don't like, not one bit. I want that scumbag. I want him soon. And I want him here, where Frank and me can show him how the Draytons pay out their retribution.'

'And you will, Charlie, believe me you will. You got my word on that too.'

'You'd better be right,' grunted the man hoarsely. 'Now where's that woman you rode in with?'

★ ★ ★

Sheriff Palmer reined his mount from the main trail to the lee of a sprawl of rocks where the moonlight was no more than a softly filtered pool of silver. He waited for the two riders following to join him, then relaxed the reins across the neck of his mount and mopped at his dust-caked face with a large bandanna.

'See anythin'?' he asked.

'Trail's as dead as dry wood,' said his powerfully built, ruddy-cheeked deputy, Sol Gibbs. 'But they passed this way, sure enough. Question is: where'd they turn off for wherever it is they're holed-up?' His dark eyes probed the night like a watchful hawk.

'We're goin' to have to wait for first light,' added Byron Byam, easing the ache in his sore buttocks. 'Or mebbe we should have brought more riders.'

'Couldn't spare 'em,' said Palmer, pocketing the bandanna. 'Need to leave as many guns as possible guardin' the town — just in case.'

'In case of what?' frowned Byam.

'In case we don't make it back,' grinned the deputy.

'Very comfortin', I'm sure,' mused Byam. 'What are we goin' to do once we've found Sheri, f'crissake? Assumin' we find her. Three of us against the Drayton gang ain't goin' to be a deal of use.'

'Four of us if McCreedy's ridin' ahead,' said Palmer.

'You figure he is?'

'Old Stoney was clear enough. No reason to doubt him.'

The deputy eased his mount beyond the pool of moonlight and stared into the dark distance of rocks and shadowy peaks. 'Time was way back when it was reckoned as how there was a fortune in silver waiting up in them hills,' he murmured. 'Nobody ever found it, leastways nobody ever said he did, but, hell, enough fools tried.'

'All very interestin', Mr Gibbs', soothed Byam, but it ain't helpin' — '

'Which gets me to wonderin',' continued Gibbs, 'if there's any place up there, some old shack or mine drift, where the Draytons might feel safe and where perhaps — '

'I see what you're gettin' at,' said Byam. 'You mean they might be holdin' Sheri in some such place. What do you think, Sheriff?'

'Soundest suggestion we've had yet,' agreed Palmer, taking up the reins. 'And you could be right, Sol. The Drayton boys are sure to have gone deep and might just have gotten lucky and stumbled into the old mine workings, or mebbe known of them. Suit their purpose ideally.' He scanned the darkness. 'Sandy Pass lies due north, and that's roughly where the hills are at their deepest.'

'So due north it is,' grinned the storekeeper before adding, 'and let's pray we ain't too late.'

★　★　★

Sheri Ward watched the darkness begin to move. It parted slowly, silently, the shape of the man seeming to melt through it like some wet, pungent substance. She backed deeper into the corner of the cabin as the door creaked closed and the shape moved on.

She blinked quickly, catching a glimpse now of the man's face, the black stubble, bulbous nose, full lips, glinting eyes. She stiffened, her hands fumbling uselessly for something, anything, to grab, perhaps as a weapon. There was nothing save the splintered roughness of the walls.

'Stand your ground there, mister,' she croaked, surprised that she had found her voice. 'Not another step.'

The shape was abruptly still. 'You goin' to make this difficult?' grunted Drayton, his gaze gleaming, a sliding grin at his lips. 'So what's the big deal? You're a bar whore, ain't yuh? Just shifted your business premises, that's all.' He wiped a lathering of sweat from his face.

'I said not another step,' croaked Sheri again.

'Oh, my,' grinned the man, 'ain't you just somethin'! And I suppose you're somehow goin' to stop me takin' that step. That the thinkin'? Well, don't waste my time, lady. I ain't for bein' messed with.'

'Me neither — and definitely not by the likes of you.'

Drayton took another step, a scowl darkening his face. 'Let's get one thing straight, lady. You ain't got no odds goin' for you right now. Not one. Nothin'. Get that clear in your head, will yuh? And then, and only then, and if I'm so minded, I might just get to keepin' you alive, leastways for as long as it takes for me and my brother Frank to finish with this godforsaken territory.'

'Go to hell, Charlie Drayton,' sneered Sheri, her eyes aching in their concentration through the pitch darkness, 'and believe me you're goin' to be makin' one almighty mistake if you're figurin' on Peppersville fallin' as easy as Leverton. Peppersville folk don't bend to nobody.'

'That so? Well, we'll see, won't we?

Meantime, don't you go botherin' that pretty head of yours with such matters. There's other things . . . '

Drayton waited, his eyes wide and gleaming, fingers flexing at his sides, the sweat beaded like frost on his stubble. Sheri backed as deep as she could push herself, wishing for the walls to swallow her, the ground to open up. She could already feel the man's breath on her face, smell the filth of his clothes, imagine the touch of his calloused hands when finally they reached for her.

Drayton's arms were lifting, the fingers on both hands set to claw the ragged remains of Sheri's dress from her body, when the cabin door opened, a shadow loomed across the splash of moonlight, and twin Colts blazed.

9

Charlie Drayton had half turned at the crashing open of the cabin door, his gunman's instincts reacting instantly to threat, a hand already closing on his holstered weapon. But the move had been split seconds behind the roaring Colts that had sent him spinning into the wall where, like a frenzied marionette, he stiffened, twitched, then slid silently to the floor.

Sheri Ward stared wide-eyed, sweat-soaked but suddenly shivering, her body detached and immobile, it seemed, from the swirl of her thoughts.

'The school teacher,' was all she could murmur.

'No time for talk, ma'am,' said McCreedy, packing his guns before grabbing Sheri's hand. 'All hell's about to break. Let's move!'

They were out of the cabin and

into the moonlit night in seconds, McCreedy heading deep into the sprawl of rocks and boulders. Sheri coughed, gasped, stumbled, the ragged dress flowing round her like black wings, the shouts of Drayton's roused men ringing in her ears.

McCreedy's grip tightened as he pushed on into the rocks, going deeper, then suddenly higher, scrambling through shale and loose stones, breaking through the darkness with the assurance of a cat.

'Where we goin'?' gasped Sheri.

'Peppersville — if our luck holds,' returned McCreedy, easing between a grip of boulders.

Sheri stumbled and looked back. 'They've found the body,' she hissed at the lift of voices from the direction of the cabin. 'They'll be followin'. No sayin' how many.'

'Enough,' said McCreedy. 'Which is why we must keep movin'.'

Sheri tossed her hair, blinked, wiped a smear of cold sweat from her face.

'Hold it,' she hissed again. 'Above you. Patch of light to your left.'

She pressed herself tight against the cold rock at her back and peered into the crags above her, watching carefully as the shadows shifted to the drifts of light. 'Do you see him?' she whispered. 'One man. He has a rifle. I saw him.'

'A lookout,' muttered McCreedy. 'We can mebbe move round him. Get clear before — '

'Too damned late. He's seen us!'

Sheri's brow gleamed on another lathering of sweat. The lookout had paused only seconds to stare once, twice to be certain he was not mistaken, before raising the Winchester to his shoulder and firing.

The shot clipped the lip of a ledge above McCreedy's head. 'Down,' he croaked, pushing Sheri lower. He ducked and glided into the deeper shadows ahead of him, one Colt drawn, his gaze riveted on the silhouetted shape of the lookout, the rifle still raised.

A second shot rang out, this time looser and shorter, scattering a sweep of shale. 'Hell!' cursed McCreedy, his gaze shifting quickly to scan the surrounds. The shooting would almost certainly bring a handful of Drayton's men his way. It would take only a matter of minutes.

He mouthed another curse, checked that the woman was still hidden in the rocks, and slid away, his eyes concentrated again as the look-out left the higher crags and made his way towards the shale.

McCreedy adjusted his grip on the Colt, narrowed his gaze and waited for the man to come on.

⋆　⋆　⋆

The Peppersville storekeeper reined his snorting, bucking mount to a halt in the shadows of the rocks and calmed it to a sweating standstill in the echo of the shots.

'Hell, did you hear that?' he croaked

as Sheriff Palmer and his deputy reined to Byam's side.

'Rifle shots. Winchester,' said Gibbs, his tight gaze moving over the night-shrouded rocks.

'Not McCreedy,' added Byam. 'He weren't packin' a rifle.'

'Somebody catchin' up with McCreedy,' grunted Palmer, patting his mount's neck.

'I figure for the shots comin' from somewhere just south of the Pass,' mused Gibbs, still scanning the rocks. 'We ain't that far away.'

'So we push on?' asked Byam.

The sheriff cleared his dusty throat. 'We get closer, but we don't go chargin' in like spooked steers. We ain't sure of the situation. Mebbe McCreedy's only been seen. Mebbe he's got to Sheri. Could be them shots were the last he ever heard. We don't know, so we go carefully, easy.'

He took a long look over the night, the streams and pools of moonlight. 'Couple of hours yet to dawn. That's to our advantage. We need the dark. But we stay close and keep it silent. If McCreedy's on the run, we ain't for hamperin' him.'

'And if he ain't?' frowned the storekeeper.

Palmer flicked his reins. 'I ain't accountin' for that — not yet.'

★ ★ ★

Three steps, four, a tentative fifth. The lookout felt for his balance on the edge of the shale slope, conscious of being exposed, a sitting target in the moon-light. He felt again, looked round him anxiously, spread his arms and moved carefully.

McCreedy ran his tongue over dry, cracked lips and tightened his gaze. The man was still too far away for a single shot to down him, but time was running out. It only needed Drayton's men to join him and McCreedy would be hopelessly outnumbered and the woman back in the hands of the gunslingers, this time with no prospect of rescue.

McCreedy grunted quietly to himself, concentrated his grip on the Colt and eased through the shadows like a snake.

It was in that moment that Sheri Ward caught her breath, shivered on the cling of the cold sweat and pressed herself tighter to the rocks. She had seen the lookout reach the shale, watched him hesitate then move on, and at the same time realized what was going through McCreedy's mind: if he waited for the man to come closer it would be too late — for both of them.

She fingered the rags of her dress nervously as her gaze followed McCreedy's every move. A shift to the left; pause, shift again; into the shadows, through them. Careful steps, watchful eyes. Pause. Crouch lower. The lookout was almost at the end of the shale bed. He was within gunshot range.

Sheri tensed, glanced quickly beyond

the lookout to the crags the lookout had left. No hint of Drayton's men, but they must be close by now, she thought, pulling a torn strip of the dress across her bruised shoulders.

The lookout had halted, uncertain of where his target lay hidden, fearful perhaps of the surprise attack that might spring from the darkness. She tensed again as she saw McCreedy grow suddenly taller, straighter in the rocks, the glint of a single Colt like a shaft of the moonlight in his hand.

The shot ripped across the night to hurl the lookout back to the shale bed as if plucked from his feet between giant fingers. The body lay still for a moment, twisted and darkening under the spread of blood, then twitched violently and slid slowly from sight, the weight of it crunching and grinding the shale on its way to the rocks.

Sheri gasped, pulled at the dress and shifted to McCreedy's waved instructions to head to the gap in the boulders to her left. She stumbled away, the first shouts of Drayton's men gathering on the darkness like the screeches of attacking hawks.

She risked a backward glance, saw McCreedy's shadow looming and fading, heard the thud and scrape of boots on rocks, the sudden rip and blaze of shots from the gunslingers as they glimpsed their first sighting of McCreedy. But the aims were high and wild, wasted lead that spat and ricocheted through the rocks.

McCreedy reached Sheri's side and grabbed her hand. 'There's a horse hitched back of that cut. Go for it,' he urged. 'Don't stop for nothin'. I'll keep these guns occupied for a while. Now shift!'

Sheri was into mouthing a protest when a blaze of shots rang out drowning her words.

McCreedy pushed her towards the cut, his eyes gleaming his insistence. 'Go,' he ordered, at the same time lifting his gaze to the rocks and ledges above him.

'McCreedy!' yelled Sheriff Palmer from his cover to the teacher's left. 'Get yourself out of there, f'crissake. There's three of us up here. We'll cover you.'

McCreedy acknowledged the sheriff with a wave, took a firmer hold of Sheri's hand and dived into the shadows of the cut, the echoes of the blazing guns ringing across the moonlit night like a fire storm.

10

Sheriff Palmer strode the length of the boardwalk fronting his office, came to a halt, blew a line of smoke from a newly lit cheroot and watched enviously as it curled into oblivion. He would give a good deal right now to be as fleeting as a line of smoke, to be free of Peppersville, the star pinned on his shirt and the responsibilities that went with the wearing of it.

But, what the hell, he thought, grunting his annoyance at the still-nagging throb in his hand, he was here, all flesh and bone, and the duly elected upholder of law and order. And it was one almighty job facing him.

He turned, paused a moment to take in the freshness of the early-morning air, and walked back to the group of men waiting at his office door.

'We were lucky — very lucky,' he said

scanning the serious faces watching him. 'Another few minutes and McCreedy would have had the whole of the Drayton gang on his neck. And that might have been too much, even for him.'

He waited a moment, taking in the tiredness in Sol Gibbs' eyes, the dusty grey of Byron Byam's pallor, the solemn air surrounding Ephraim Judd, the already florid glow on Clyde Harte's face. 'As it was,' he went on, blowing another line of smoke, 'we all got clear, rode like the wind for town, and made it. Doc Walker's with Sheri Ward and McCreedy right now. And don't nobody fret on one score: Sheri's goin' to be fine in a day or so.'

'Thanks to McCreedy,' added Harte, wiping his face.

'McCreedy . . . ' mused the undertaker quietly, his pince-nez glinting in the strengthening sunlight. 'The man's a mystery. We still know nothin' of him; who he is, where he comes from; why he's tied in with somebody called M.S., and more to the point, why he's here.'

'All in good time, all in good time,' counselled Palmer with a flourish of the cheroot. 'We got other matters to consider. Important matters that ain't goin' to wait.'

Byam dusted the dirt from his coat. 'Spell 'em out, though I reckon I know what's comin'.'

'Figure it,' began the sheriff, 'why didn't the Drayton mob ride us down out of Sandy Pass? They could have. They had the mounts, fresh and rested. They had the numbers, and no sayin' to how many. And they sure as hell had good cause. McCreedy had just shot Charlie Drayton and whipped Sheri from under their very noses. So why did they let us go?'

'Tell me,' sweated Harte, 'much as I don't want to hear it.'

'I'll tell you why,' said Palmer, 'because Frank Drayton reckons on exacting his own version of retribution. That's why. Him and his scumbags are goin' to ride in and take Peppersville apart. They ain't goin' to leave nothin' and mebbe nobody standin' — and they ain't goin' to be long in gettin' to it.'

'How long we got?' croaked Harte.

'We'd only be guessin',' clipped Judd, adjusting his pince-nez. 'Real question we've got to ask is: where are we goin' to get help, and how fast can we raise it?'

'That ain't goin' to be anythin' like easy,' said Sol Gibbs, relaxing his weight to one hip as he folded his arms. 'You'd have to be lookin' at a big town for the sorta help we're goin' to need, and there ain't one under a hundred miles distant. There wouldn't be the time to get there, raise the guns and get back. There'd be nothin' to come back to.'

'Telegraph,' beamed Harte. 'We could use the wire to summon help. That's the answer.'

'No telegraph here,' returned Palmer. 'Nearest would be at North Rocks. Too far away.'

'So what do we do?' persisted Harte. 'Can't just sit around waitin' for Drayton to pick his time, f'crissake. That ain't no option, never has been, leastways not in my book. But we ain't got a hope in hell's chance of standin' and fightin' if we ain't got guns. And the sorta guns we're lookin' for ain't in exactly plentiful supply. So, like I say — '

'Hear well enough what you're sayin', Clyde,' the sheriff interrupted, finishing the cheroot and flicking the butt to the dirt. 'You ain't sayin' nothin' new.'

'Fact is, though,' persisted Byam, 'there'll be folk packin' up and leavin' town if we ain't seen to be doin' somethin'. Gettin' Sheri back from the Draytons was one thing, but the threat in the takin' was another. And folk ain't goin' to bury their heads against what's comin' next. They'll know. They ain't fools.'

The storekeeper ran a finger round the sweaty cling of his collar. 'We got lucky out there at the Pass, sure enough, but where's our luck leadin' us now?'

★ ★ ★

Luck, or more probably Fate, led Sheriff Palmer later that morning to the quiet of his private room at the rear of his office where, with the drapes drawn against the glare of the sunlight, he lay on his bed and closed his eyes.

The ride to Sandy Pass, the rescue of Sheri and the skirmish with the Drayton gang had taken their toll on his already weary body and racing thoughts. Now, in the silence and sticky warmth of the small room, the images clamoured again, the doubts, the fears, the pitiable prospect facing Preacher Peabody. Questions pounded through his mind in a crazed stampede.

Who was McCreedy? The whole town needed to know, to talk to him. But had the shooting of Reights and Jones only worsened matters?

Where had McCreedy come from? Where had he learned to handle twin Colts like a professional? And who was M.S.?

When would Frank Drayton attack? How could the town defend itself? Where . . .

The sheriff had drifted into a fitful sleep, the throbbing ache in his hand bringing him to the surface in spasms of twitching and sweating, until on a long grumbling sigh, he had resolved to get back to his office, call a meeting of the leading town men and come to some firm decisions.

Twenty minutes later he was awake, aware of a movement, a presence in the soft gloom. He tensed, but stayed where he was, eyes wide, staring for a moment at the ceiling then more watchfully through the area he could scan from where he lay.

There was someone in the room.

★ ★ ★

'How the hell did you get in?' groaned Palmer, struggling to support himself on one elbow, blinking into the shadowy gloom like an owl.

'Backdoor wasn't locked,' said the man, a soft smile brightening his eyes. 'Kinda careless at a time like this, Sheriff.'

'I don't need remindin' on that score, McCreedy,' snorted Palmer, finally managing to swing his legs from the bed. 'But as you know well enough, I've been a mite busy just lately.'

McCreedy shifted a foot. 'Glad you were around when you were. Things were gettin' a touch hot out there at the Pass. I'm grateful to you and that goes for the lady too.'

'That's all very well, McCreedy,' began Palmer again, coming to his feet, 'but there's a whole heap of questions concernin' you that have got to be answered before this next hour's through. Damn it, I've got a town out there that's just about to get as out of hand as a mad dog if somethin' ain't done soon to protect it against the Drayton threat.'

The sheriff reached for his gunbelt and buckled it defiantly at his waist. 'And frankly, McCreedy, if you want the blunt truth of it, I ain't got a notion worth spittin' on of how we're goin' to save the dirt, never mind lives and buildings. Once them Drayton boys . . . ' The lawman's eyes narrowed in their concentration on the face in the shadows. 'But I don't have to tell you about the Drayton gang, do I? You've already crossed 'em, and mebbe more than once. That so?'

There were sounds of activity in the office beyond the private room; the banging of a door, heavy footfalls, and then Sol Gibbs' voice raised in an urgent call. 'We got company, Sheriff. Best get yourself out here.'

11

The main street had filled with a jostling, clamouring crowd of folk, men, women and children of all ages, some still hugging the shadowed safety of the boardwalk, others already gathering in small groups, talking, shouting, gesturing, while the majority had circled the object of their noisy attention: the blood-soaked body of deputy Sam Denver, dumped face-down in the dirt.

'What the hell's goin' on here?' growled Sheriff Palmer, pushing and elbowing this way through the crowd, McCreedy and Sol Gibbs in his wake. 'What's happened, f'crissake?'

'It's Sam — he's dead, right here at my feet,' called a man fronting the throng round the body.

'Rider came in from Sandy Pass way,' shouted another. 'Had Sam's body slung across his mount. Just tossed the poor devil to the ground and kept right on goin'. Sonofabitch!'

'Anybody recognize the rider?' asked Palmer, standing over the body as Doc Walker finally got to examining it.

'Didn't have to recognize the rat,' cursed a man from the boardwalk. 'One of Drayton's men. Got to be.'

The throng chorused its agreement.

'Retribution!'

'That's what we get for shootin' up them gunslingers.'

'We hang about here much longer they'll get us all, every last man.'

Another chorus of agreement greeted the voice. A child sobbed. A dog barked.

'How come they got to Sam anyhow?' shouted a youth, waving a clenched fist. 'We should go teach them sons-of-goddamn-bitches some lessons!'

'Hold up there,' growled Palmer again, raising his arm for quiet. 'Just hold it, will yuh?' He waited, his gaze glaring over the faces surrounding him. 'Sam Denver was doin' his job as a good and trusted deputy. He had volunteered — *volunteered*, do yuh hear? — to keep a watch on the main trail out of the Pass. He was due to report in mid-afternoon. Sol here would've replaced him.' Palmer paused, his gaze still on the faces as they eased from their anger and settled in quiet thought. 'Sam was a good man,' he went on gently. 'One of the best. Committed to the law and this town and you folk.'

'That's all very well,' clipped a man in the main throng. 'Ain't nobody denyin' that Sam wasn't decent and law-abidin', but, hell, Sheriff, he's lyin' dead here. Shot down in cold blood by them Drayton scum. You ain't sayin' as how we ain't got no right to react to that, are yuh?'

The crowd began to stir and murmur again.

' 'Course I ain't,' shouted Palmer above the swelling voices. 'He was my deputy, damnit. But that ain't — '

'Preacher Peabody, then Sheri, and

now Sam. Who's next?'

'Yeah, who's next?' added another voice. 'You, me, my wife, one of the kids here?'

The throng began to shift and clamour again.

'I'll tell yuh what we should be doin',' the voice persisted. 'I'll spell it out — '

A single shot cracked across the stifling, shimmering air. 'No, I'll spell it out,' called McCreedy, stepping up to the boardwalk, a Colt still smoking in his hand. 'And you'll listen up, every last one of you.'

* * *

The gathering in the hot, dusty street fell silent. Men flourished bandannas to mop at the sweat on their agitated faces. Mothers drew young ones to their skirts. The barking dog slunk away to the shadows. Somebody produced a blanket to cover the body. Flies buzzed.

'Let's hear the man,' ordered the sheriff.

'Let's do that,' echoed the old-timer. 'Damnit, we owe the fella some already. Least we can do is hear him.'

The crowd murmured approvingly.

'And let's get to it before them scumbags show their faces again,' urged a man shielding his eyes against the glare.

'Or dump another body on us,' persisted another, spitting angrily.

'Let's have some order, f'crissake,' shouted Byron Byam, surprised at the sudden authority in his voice. 'It's only decent,' he added quietly.

McCreedy holstered the Colt with a slap. 'They won't be back,' he said, 'leastways not yet awhile.'

'You sound awfully sure about that, mister,' retorted Clyde Harte from the depths of a cloud of cigar smoke. 'How come?'

The undertaker tapped his pince-nez. 'It's a fair point, sir,' he murmured. 'You're voicin' an opinion there I can't rightly appreciate from where I'm standin'.' He glanced quickly at the covered body.

'Appreciate what you're sayin', Mr Judd, but I know these fellas,' continued McCreedy. 'I've known the Draytons a long time. Too long.'

The gathering stirred and began to murmur. Doc Walker's gaze on the man narrowed to a thoughtful stare. Sheriff Palmer brushed at an irritating fly. Byam and the undertaker exchanged glances. Clyde Harte blew thick smoke and coughed.

'I ain't for goin' into the details right now,' said McCreedy, scanning the watching faces. 'They ain't relevant. Just take it from me that my figurin' on what Frank Drayton will do next ain't goin' to be far short of the mark.'

The crowd began to murmur again. The sheriff was hearing voices: echoes of Preacher Peabody's description of what he had found in McCreedy's room, Ephraim Judd's theory on the meaning of the map and telegraph wire,

Sheri Ward's fears . . .

'So just what will the rats do?' croaked a barrel-chested man, wiping the sweat from his neck.

'They ain't for lettin' us be, that's for sure,' said a skinny youth at his side. 'They ain't that dumb.'

The gathering agreed.

McCreedy raised a hand for silence. 'They ain't dumb, far from it, but they ain't that predictable neither. The Draytons have always been their own men, Frank especially. He's the thinker, the one who plots out the next move. Cunnin' as a fox, deadly as a rattler. And he's the last of the brothers, so whatever he's got planned for Peppers-ville is goin' to be some occasion.'

There was a moment's silence when even the flies were still, when faces drained, sweat gleamed, eyes simply stared.

'It's like we said, we gotta do somethin',' called a voice breaking the quiet. 'And we'd better start now. No messin'!'

The throng came to life again.

'He's right. Let's do somethin'!'

'Take the fight to 'em, is what I say. Every man rides out to Sandy Pass.'

'Shoot the hell out of the vermin.'

'Don't leave nobody standin'. Not one.'

'Save some for hangin'!'

'And we'll string 'em up right here in town. Ain't a livin' soul goin' to forget what Peppersville stood for.'

The throng cheered. McCreedy's Colt blazed again.

'That's fool talk,' snapped the teacher. 'Do any of that and you're dead men, all of you. If you want to save this town and your lives you'll take the only course open to you: pack enough belongin's as is necessary, and leave. We'll turn Peppersville into a ghost town, then come back to haunt it.'

12

The light faded quickly that day to a dusk that hung grey and silent. Night would settle early, but it was a cover welcomed by the townsfolk of Peppersville as they went about the misery of preparing to vacate their homes.

They had gone along with McCreedy's advice almost without dissent.

'Won't be for long, anyhow,' the old-timer had reasoned. 'And if it saves lives . . . well, there ain't no argument, is there? We pack what we need, then sneak out of town like snuffle-nosed cats.'

'I'm all for lookin' to my wife and young 'uns and doin' the best by them,' a younger man had agreed. 'But, hell, it's some prospect, ain't it? Supposin' — '

'No supposin',' the old man had argued. 'Let's get ourselves to Drift

Creek as fast as we can. Ain't nobody goin' to look for us there. We'll settle best we can under canvas, in wagons where we got 'em, and there's any number of dry caves along the creek. No shortage of timber either.' He had smacked his lips enthusiastically. 'Yessir, be just like the old days when we got to settlin' this territory. Why, I recall . . . '

Sheriff Palmer, on the other hand, pacing the length of his crowded, smoke-hazed office where the glow from a single lantern cast giant shadows across the walls, had his own doubts about the venture.

'It's one helluva gamble,' he said, turning to the faces watching him. 'Gettin' to the creek under the cover of darkness might just be possible, providin' we stay organized and move real quiet. It's what we do later that bothers me. And we still don't know anythin' like enough about McCreedy.'

'Mebbe we should come clean and tell him what Preacher Peabody found in his room,' suggested Byam, fingering the lapels of his coat. 'Heck, if we're puttin' this much trust in the fella and his advice, then surely . . . '

'That's nothin' to what he's askin' us to leave behind,' blustered the saloon-keeper, fumbling to light another cigar. 'Think about it: your store, Byron, my whole business; the livery, Ephraim's parlour, and that's without reckonin' on the homes. If the Drayton gang gets to lootin' and ransackin' and then torchin' the whole shebang, what we goin' to be left with, f'crissake? We'll have lost everythin'.'

'Except our lives,' said Doc Walker quietly from his seat at the sheriff's desk. 'You ain't for book-keepin' them in your ledgers of loss, are you, Clyde?' Doc's stare was defiant. ' 'Course you ain't. You can't put a price on a life. So let the Drayton mob do their worst. If we survive, we've won.'

Ephraim Judd cleared his throat and adjusted his pince-nez. ''Ceptin' I don't see Mr McCreedy optin' for doin' nothin'. He spoke back there of creatin' a ghost town, then returnin' to haunt it. And I figure for him havin' precisely that in mind.'

'Some teacher!' mocked Byam. 'How come — '

'Don't ask,' said the sheriff raising his good hand. 'I ain't got the time or the inclination. Let's just get to clearin' this town. Questions surroundin' McCreedy are goin' to have to wait, save one: where is he now?'

'Up at the livery with Old Stoney,' said deputy Gibbs at the window.

'Right,' continued Palmer, 'so let's do some plannin' and shiftin'. Get them girls of yours organized, Clyde. Mebbe Sheri's up to helpin'. Take what you can load from the store, Byron. Food, spare clothes, blankets. Water ain't goin' to be no problem. Creek's brimmin' even in this heat.' He crossed to his desk. 'Goin' to have to leave Preacher Peabody in your hands, Doc. Do your best for him, but he's goin' to have to be moved, however painful.'

Doc Walker nodded, came to his feet and disappeared into the night.

'Organize lookouts to watch the trail into town, Sol,' the sheriff went on, turning to his gun cabinet. 'And you, Ephraim, can take charge of whatever we can raise in the way of rifles, sidearms and ammunition.'

'Got a pine coffin back at the parlour that'll hold 'em just fine,' smiled the undertaker settling his pince-nez again. 'Ain't that just a stroke of good fortune?'

★　★　★

Peppersville emptied slowly, silently that night like a barrel being carefully drained of its contents. Folk moved quickly but efficiently under the cover of darkness where the only lights were the few soft glows from trimmed lamps and drifts of moonlight through a cloud-scudded sky.

Wagons came out of dusty retirement, teams were found to haul them, tack sometimes long-since put aside was cleaned and polished. The few possessions finally selected, loaded and secured were practical, the everyday articles that ensured survival; some were personal, especially where children were concerned and, in the case of the old-timer's rocking chair, an obstinate refusal to be parted from a 'friend'.

It was an hour after midnight, with the air thin and chill and some folk welcoming the comfort of a spare blanket thrown across the shoulders, when Sheriff Palmer, Byron Byam, Doc Walker, Ephraim Judd, Clyde Harte and McCreedy watched intently as Old Stoney made his final inspection of the outfits drawn up in the main street.

'They're as ready to roll as they'll ever be,' he pronounced, wiping his hands on a grease-stained rag. 'They'll make it.'

'Good,' said Palmer with a satisfied grunt. He turned to McCreedy. 'You satisfied, mister? Best we can do.'

McCreedy nodded from where he

waited in the shadows.

'Never thought I'd live to see such a day,' murmured the storekeeper through a deep sigh. 'Just don't seem right.'

'You can say that again,' agreed Harte, pulling his waistcoat over his ample girth. 'It's no better than runnin' away.'

'But it's a whole sight better than fillin' Boot Hill with dead bodies,' snapped Doc, his eyes flashing. 'Don't like this any more than you do, but I ain't for seein' them families out there fallin' to the guns of Frank Drayton and his rats.' He glanced quickly at McCreedy. 'And besides, this might just work.'

'Sure as hell would give a lot to see the look on Drayton's face when he rides in,' chuckled Sol Gibbs. 'Sight for sore eyes that'll be.'

'Yeah, well, that ain't our concern right now,' said the sheriff, stepping from the boardwalk to join Old Stoney. 'Time's come to get these wagons movin'. We need to make all the miles we can before dawn. So let's roll!'

The line pulled out at an even, gentle pace with the minimum of fuss and sound; no shouted orders, no urging of the teams save with the click of a tongue, a flick of the reins, snap of tack. Wheels and timbers creaked, leather strained under heavy weights, hoofs scuffed through the dirt, horses snorted, dogs padded in the wake of movement. Shadows leapt and settled. The night deepened. Moonlight merely watched.

Some of the womenfolk dabbed fitfully at tearful eyes and hugged the young ones to them. Some looked straight ahead, others risked awkward glances back as if to record a particular shape or place, some simply to recall.

The old-timer spat and tugged at the brim of his hat. 'Make no mistake,' he grunted as Old Stoney drew his mount alongside the outfit, 'we'll be back — and you can bet to that. Yessir. Them Drayton scum might have an edge right now, but that ain't to say they'll hold to it.' He spat again and flicked the reins to his team. 'We'll sure as hell be back!'

'That's the spirit,' smiled the livery owner moving on down the line. 'Just keep 'em rollin' nice and easy.'

Sheri Ward gave the looming bulk of the Broken Nugget no more than a half-hearted glance from her place with the bar girls in Clyde Harte's open wagon. She could hope it might be her last sight of the building and the town, but she had her doubts. She shivered in the night chill and snuggled into the shawl across her shoulders, the sudden recollections of the hours spent in the shack at Sandy Pass flooding in a jumble of images: the cobwebbed window, the gleam in snake-face's eyes, the look on Charlie Drayton's face, his body sliding like a mass of mud to the floor.

And then of McCreedy, the Colts in his hands. She shivered again. Where was the man, she wondered, peering anxiously into the passing shadows . . .

'One minute that McCreedy fella's there, the next he's gone, like a mist to a breeze.' The storekeeper shook his head. 'Still, can't be waitin' on him right now. Got to be movin', get this wagon load of stores to the creek along of the folk. See you there, Ephraim.'

'O'course,' answered Judd. 'See you at the creek.'

The undertaker settled his pince-nez, shrugged his shoulders into the folds of his coat and made his way towards his mount. It was true, he pondered, McCreedy was like a mist to a breeze; there, somewhere in the shadows, watching, waiting.

But where was he waiting now, and who was he watching?

13

There was already the softest glow of the new dawn light when the first of the wagons out of Peppersville left the main trail heading South and swung east towards Drift Creek.

Sheriff Palmer reined his mount to the side of Doc Walker's outfit and rode easy. 'How's the preacher?' he asked, glancing to what he could see of the covered wagon's dark interior.

'Makin' out best he can,' said Doc, encouraging the team to the rougher scrub. 'Sleepin' right now. One of the women is nursin' him. He'll make it.' He flicked the reins and clicked his tongue. 'Any sign of McCreedy?'

'Not so much as a whisper. I figure he's mebbe stayed behind, keepin' an eye on the place for a while. He'll show up when he's good and ready.'

Doc studied the rough track and

surrounding scrub for a moment. 'Sure got one hell of a heap of questions to put to that fella,' he mused. 'When I get the chance! Damn it, I ain't never come across anybody so elusive. Goes his own way at the drop of a hat. Meantime — '

'Meantime, we get these folk settled and our priorities in order,' said Palmer, pulling his collar into his neck on the nip of the early-morning air. 'First thing is to ensure a ready supply of water and fuel for the fires. Then we secure the place. Post lookouts on a rota basis usin' all the men we can spare. I ain't anticipatin' the Drayton boys ridin' in here, but I ain't for takin' risks — which is why we're goin' to need eyes watchin' the town. We've got to know what's goin' on there. I'll be callin' for volunteers to ride along of myself and Sol.'

'And McCreedy, what about him?' asked Doc. 'If you're goin' to keep an eye on anybody, it's mebbe him you should be watchin'.'

The sheriff grunted, narrowed his

gaze on the spreading dawn light and tightened his grip on the reins. 'I ain't for chasin' shadows at this point,' he murmured. 'I got all I can handle right now.'

★ ★ ★

The light was brighter and stronger some hours later when the trail out of the crags and peaks heading due south thundered to the beat of hoofs as Frank Drayton led his gang of gunslingers into Peppersville. They rode without pausing, at the same heated pace, the mounts round-eyed and anxious, their riders intent and unremitting.

They numbered more than twenty, rough, hard-drinking, fast-shooting men who cared nothing for the past, very little for the future and lived only for whatever could be prised, stolen, looted or beaten from the day wherever it happened to dawn. They rode on the orders of their leader, surviving and thriving because of and by the gun.

They knew no law save the strange, unwritten code of honour that existed among themselves.

Frank Drayton, a sour-faced but keen-eyed man, with a twitchy nerve beneath an ugly cheek scar, led the fast-riding bunch that morning, flanked to his left and right by his two most trusted lieutenants since the loss of his brothers.

Myers Forman — the snake-faced man who had abducted Sheri Ward — was the senior of the two, a long-standing gunslinger, bank robber and gun for hire wherever the price was right. Sharing Frank's trust was Boyd Knapp, a quiet, softly spoken, philosophizing killer with a specialist ability in the handling of knives. Both men had ridden with the Drayton brothers for the best part of five years and were considered, in Frank's roughshod code of conduct, to be 'partners'.

It was a few minutes after eight o'clock with the sun climbing, the heat thickening and the flies pestering, when the gang finally rode into the deserted town.

* * *

'Gone! There ain't a livin' soul in sight. Not so much as a dog.' Myers Forman thudded to the bar of the Broken Nugget, helped himself to a bottle of whiskey, opened it and gulped angrily at the contents. 'Place is deserted,' he growled, thrusting the cork back to the bottle. 'So what the hell's goin' on here?' He swung his flashing stare from Boyd Knapp to Drayton. 'What yuh reckon, Frank?'

'I reckon,' said the man, tracing a finger across the surface of the table in front of him, 'that I might just have acquired myself a whole town.'

The handful of Drayton's men lounging round the saloon began to titter. Knapp cleaned his fingernails with the point of a knife.

'Mebbe yuh have at that,' growled

Forman again, 'but this ain't one bit natural, is it? Where have the folk gone? I can figure why they've packed up and left — that ain't difficult — but *all* of them? Every last man, just pulled out like rats in a flood. Damnit, there's still smoke comin' from the livery forge!' He turned to the bottle again and drew the cork. 'Let me tell you somethin', Frank, we've ridden into a ghost town.'

The men shifted uncomfortably and murmured among themselves. Boyd Knapp thrust the knife to its scabbard and crossed to the batwings.

Drayton continued to trace the tabletop. 'So what you sayin' there, Myers?' he asked without lifting his sullen gaze. 'You tellin' me we got some trouble here or somethin'? You sayin' we can't handle this?'

''Course I ain't,' smiled Forman. 'Ain't sayin' nothin' like that. Hell, there ain't nothin' we can't handle. All I'm sayin' is what we got here ain't as we reckoned.'

Drayton shrugged. 'I ain't complainin', am I? I don't see none of the boys complainin'. Boyd there ain't complainin'. All I'm hearin' is you mouthin' on.'

'Now hold up there — ' protested Forman, thudding the bottle back to the bar.

'No, my friend, you hold up.' Drayton's finger came to rest as he lifted his stare, the nerve twitching restlessly behind his scar. 'I'll tell you what we do here. Spell it out in full so you won't be troubled no more. We help ourselves, Myers. As simple as that. We've got a bar here; clean sheets and proper beds anywhere we care to choose 'em; we've got our own store, our own livery . . . damnit, there ain't nothin' we ain't got. So, like I say, we help ourselves. Rest up awhile. Take it easy. Eat well, drink all we want, sleep when we feel the need for as long as it pleases. All we're missin' is some women, but mebbe we'll get to solvin' that.'

Drayton drummed his fingers quietly, rhythmically on the table, the nerve behind the scar beginning to settle, the stare unblinking. 'If folk get to bein' fool enough to hand me a town, I ain't for declinin' the offer. I take it. And I have.'

★   ★   ★

And like some warrior surveying an addition to his empire, Frank Drayton spent much of the rest of that day proving that he had indeed 'taken' the town of Peppersville.

He strutted the boardwalks with the largesse of newly acquired wealth, his lieutenants and men following dutifully in his steps. 'Help yourself to shirts and pants, boys, boots too if you've a fancy,' he had gestured on reaching Byron Byam's mercantile. 'Take what fits, and what don't if you reckon you can sell it!'

Homes had been looted of whatever was of value or practical use and could be carried away. Food and drink had been consumed in ever-increasing quantities until stomachs were bloated and heads reeling. When finally a particular gunslinger had sobered up enough to ask how long they might be staying in Peppersville, Drayton had eyed the man like a mountain leopard disturbed at its supper. ''Til I say other,' he had croaked. 'And when there ain't nothin' of this two-bits place worth the spittin' on. Then, my friend, we'll saddle up and ride.' He had let a grin slide round his lips. 'But not before we've watched the place burn to a cinder!'

Only one man that day had stayed indifferent to the latest Drayton conquest.

Boyd Knapp had spent much of his time taking a closer look at the town, watching it, pondering on the deeper reasons behind its being so suddenly and hurriedly deserted.

He had wandered behind the main street, taking careful note of the scuffings in the dirt, of what had obviously been removed from ramshackle outbuildings and barns; paused occasionally to study a doorway, a window in closer detail until, with a mild grunt of satisfaction, he had moved on again.

He had paused too from time to time to simply listen for the sounds beyond the whoops, shouts and drunken laughter of the gunslingers, but heard nothing, it seemed, to explain the lurking doubts in his mind.

The darkness had fallen and thickened, the night air turned lifeless and balmy, and a silence descended among the exhausted revellers sprawled in sleep in the bar, when he had strolled quietly into the deeper shadows to smoke a last cheroot of the day. Only then, in the flickering glow of a struck match, had his doubts been confirmed.

Only then had he seen the shape.

14

'He ain't shown, so I ain't waitin'. We ride at first light.' Sheriff Palmer threw the dregs of his coffee to the dirt, replaced the mug on the stones fronting the fire, and gazed tiredly into the depths of the night.

'Well, mebbe it ain't quite what it seems,' reflected Byam, shifting uncomfortably on the rock slab.

'Meanin' what?' croaked the sheriff.

'Meanin' he's mebbe got delayed or somethin'. Any one of a dozen reasons. Hell, I don't know any more than you, but I ain't for assumin' he's pulled out and just left us. That wouldn't fit with the fella I figure him for.'

'Could be he's still in town,' offered Sol Gibbs from the shadows. 'That'd be in keepin'.'

'Risky, but highly likely in my view,' said Doc Walker from behind a mug of steaming coffee.

Clyde Harte rummaged through his pockets for a cigar, found one and lit it with a taper from the fire. 'Doin' what in town precisely?' he wheezed on an intake of smoke. 'Damnit, don't take much imagination to figure what's goin' on back there. Can see it now: them scumbags'll be helpin' themselves, raidin' and lootin' like a horde of starved vermin. Won't be nothin' safe. Not a thing. And as for the Nugget . . . I daren't think.' He blew a cloud of smoke. 'Good thing we got the women clear. They're about the only thing they ain't got.'

'Yet,' murmured Ephraim Judd, peering over his pince-nez. 'Won't be long before they get to lookin' round for female diversions.'

'Mebbe, but they sure ain't goin' to find 'em here,' snapped Palmer. 'Damned if they will! We'll have this whole mess sorted by then. You can bet to it.'

'Admire your guts, Sheriff,' said Doc,

'but I ain't so sure about the prospects facin' us. Not without some word from McCreedy. Seems to me our next move should be on his sayin'.'

'You reckonin' on us just sittin' here waitin' for the man to show up?' grunted Palmer.

Doc adjusted the set of his dusty coat. 'Give it 'til noon, eh? If McCreedy ain't here by then, we do as you say and ride for town.' He looked round the faces of the others. 'We agreed?'

There were low grunts and murmurings of approval.

'The only sensible thing we can do,' said Byam.

'We owe it to McCreedy,' offered Judd.

'He'll show,' smiled Gibbs.

'He'd better,' grimaced Harte.

★　★　★

Boyd Knapp had waited only long enough for the smoke from his cheroot to drift across the night air before

130

moving quickly, silently to where the shape had paused before melting into the darkness.

No doubt now, he thought, slipping through the boardwalk shadows like a snake, one of the town men had stayed behind; one man alone was watching, noting, perhaps with a plan to report back to a larger force gathered somewhere down the trail, hidden in the hills or any one of the deeper creeks. Had they ridden into a trap? Had Frank Drayton been duped, was he even now in his drunken stupor caught like a fly in a web? He had led the gang into a ghost town that might yet prove to be a coffin.

He slid on, crossing between boardwalks without a sound, peering through tight, narrowed eyes into the blankets of darkness, identifying the shapes of the old shacks, a sprawl of barrels, piles of crates, discarded timbers, pausing every few yards to listen for the slightest sound, the merest hint of a footstep. There had been nothing.

Maybe he should wake Forman, or Drayton, get himself some help. Maybe they should scour the town until whoever was out there was caught. But maybe not, he thought. What use would a bunch of bleary-eyed drunks be?

He was approaching the livery at the far end of town, a black brooding bulk where there was still a slow wisp of smoke curling from the forge like a dying breath. He came on slowly, the steps careful, the eyes watchful, the fingers of his right hand feeling for the handle of his knife. He paused again, tensed, instinctively aware of another presence, somebody lurking somewhere.

He drew the blade from his belt, the weight of it familiar in his grip, then moved on step by step, slipping round the body of the forge, his eyes probing like white beams for anything that seemed out of place or shifted. Another step, the hand clutching the knife held lower now but still balanced ahead of him, poised to slash or stab instantly.

More steps as if on cat's paws edging him clear of the forge and towards the deeper, darker interior of the livery stabling. A half-step, a scuff of his boot through stragglings of chopped straw, sawdust and dirt. A moment to pause again, watch, listen, feel the touch of a cold sweat in his neck, and then without warning, without a sound, the flash of a bright light, the searing pain erupting, it seemed to fire in the back of his head.

He stumbled forward under the blow, the fingers of his left hand clutching blindly for a hold, scrambling on nothing more than empty space as his legs began to buckle, the fire in his head to flare, his eyes to bulge, mouth to open.

He tried to make out a shape, to turn to where he thought his attacker had struck, but now there were only shadows, the pitch darkness and the burning light in his head.

It was as he was falling that the second blow struck like the snap and crack of lightning across the hand still holding the knife. Knapp heard the splinter of bone, saw for a moment the blacksmith's hammer raised above him for a second blow, mouthed what he thought was a scream and lost consciousness on the sound of iron cleaving the air as the hammer crashed again on the knife hand and crushed it.

The dying curl of smoke from the forge hovered like a shroud.

* * *

Frank Drayton's rumbling belch from the depths of his stomach woke the man sleeping in the chair opposite him with a grunted start and grimace. His eyes opened slowly, like a shaky hand fumbling with drapes; he slapped his lips, grimaced again and struggled to sit upright.

Water. He needed water, he decided. Cool water, and plenty of it. He came unsteadily to his feet, shushing himself to silence at the creak and scrape of his chair, blinked on the still smoky haze in the saloon and made his way on tiptoed steps through the sprawled bodies to the batwings.

The dry night air smelled good, clean and fresher now in the early hours to dawn. He breathed deeply, rubbed his knuckles into his eyes and grunted. It had been a long night of free-flowing drink and all the pillaged food a man could eat. Only thing missing in this one-eyed, ghost town had been the women. But Frank had already promised to remedy that before the gang moved on. And he would. Yessir, if Frank Drayton promised, the promise would be kept.

Meantime — water. Where in the hell had the Peppersville folk stored their water?

He eased a batwing open just wide enough to slip through to the boardwalk, checked that its creak back into place had not disturbed the snoring sleepers, and stepped down to the street.

He stretched, shrugged his shoulders and peered to his left to the silent bulk of the deserted livery. Sure to be water there, he thought, wiping the back of his hand across his mouth. He turned his gaze to the right and the backdrop of hills and mountains at Sandy Pass.

It was then that he saw the water trough only steps away from where he was standing. Close, cool and beckoning. He smiled softly to himself. What the hell, water was water when it came to the need. Who cared where you found it? The trough was a whole sight closer than the livery, so the trough it would be.

The man had been splashing the water into his face, sating his thirst and cooling the harsh dryness in his throat for fully three minutes when he became conscious of the quiet crunch of a step behind him. He slapped another wave of the trough water across his cheeks and brow, shook his head and turned to greet whoever had followed him from the bar.

'Sure as hell makes a fella feel human again,' he grinned, licking his lips as he blinked on the haze in his eyes. He shook his head again, the water spraying like rain across the dirt at his feet, then peered closer. 'Who is that?' he croaked. 'That you Mace?'

The dark looming figure had closed suddenly, plunging the sidekick into shadow, his eyes wide, white and staring, wet face and lips gleaming in the vague shafts of light.

'Who the devil — ' he began, but was silenced instantly on the flash of a hand to his throat, the grip tightening like rock. The sheer strength of the figure spun the man round and plunged his head back into the trough.

There were moments then of a deep gurgling, of the man struggling against the force that held him in a merciless grip, but the hold did not weaken or loosen until the once-thirsty sidekick lay lifeless in the slowly settling water.

Only then did McCreedy dry his hands with a satisfied grunt, pause briefly to gaze over the deserted street and melt silently back to the shadows.

15

Sheriff Palmer put a finger to his lips for silence, counted out a long ten seconds, then gestured for deputy Gibbs to join him in the deepest of the noon day shadows.

'Nothin',' he hissed. 'Not a sound. What they all doin' — sleepin' it off?'

Gibbs crouched lower in the shade and cover of the ramshackle shack among the timber stores and logs on the edge of town. 'Very likely,' he agreed, squinting into the deserted, sunlit street. 'We goin' to get closer, or ain't you for riskin' it?'

'Got to,' grunted Palmer. 'We ain't come this far to go back empty-handed.'

The two men were silent for a moment. 'No hint out there of McCreedy,' said Gibbs, blinking on the sweat across his eyebrows. 'You wouldn't be for reckonin' on him havin' pulled out, would you? Just wouldn't figure.'

Palmer wiped a hand across his mouth. 'Who's to say?' he murmured. 'And, frankly, Sol, I ain't for givin' the matter too much consideration right now. We've got a town out there that's been grabbed from under our noses, and we've got the folk whose town it is camped in some godforsaken creek wonderin' if they've got any sort of a future.' The hand slewed across his mouth again. 'No, Sol, McCreedy can wait. I think we've got our priorities.'

The deputy nodded, fingered the butt of his holstered Colt and set his focus tight on the street again. 'Know somethin',' he said quietly, 'I figure for Drayton and his boys bein' holed up in the saloon. Take a look.' He waited for Palmer's gaze to sharpen on the Broken Nugget. 'Curl of smoke from the 'wings,' continued Gibbs. 'Nothin' else in sight.'

'Council of war?' asked the sheriff.

Gibbs spat a fount of spittle to within a whisker of a pestering fly. 'My guess would be they're still tryin' to fathom how it is they've ridden into a ghost town, and what to do with it now they've got it.'

Sheriff Palmer cleared his throat. 'Well, mebbe you're right, but meantime we've come this far; horses are hitched safe enough, so what say we take a closer look at this sonofabitch 'ghost' town of ours? Could be McCreedy was right. Mebbe somebody has been back to haunt it.'

★　★　★

They slid away from the shack like bodies squirming under the skin of sand and dirt, shadow to shadow, cover to cover until they were within close sight of the bar's back door.

'We goin' on?' whispered Sol, his fingers hovering again round his holster. 'Clyde ain't much for security. Back door's usually the bolt-hole for fellas who shouldn't be seein' the gals. Never locked. You want me to check?'

'Check,' said the sheriff bluntly. 'I'll cover you.'

Sol nodded, tapped the butt of his Colt and eased away to the next patch of shadow. He waited, watched, judged the distance to be covered and was all for making his move when the door opened on a creaking flurry.

Sol dropped like a stone behind the cover of an empty barrel as two sidekicks staggered and yawned their way into the sunlight, their eyes squinting on the glare, arms raised against it, tongues working feverishly on dried lips and liquor-parched throats.

The fatter, thicker-set of the two drew back to the shade at the side of the door and slumped his shoulders against the clapboard wall. 'Hell,' he groaned, 'you ain't goin' to tell me Frank was reckonin' for this.'

His partner, some years younger, leaner, with a mean, hungry glint in his eyes, thrust his hands into the side slit pockets of his pants, sank his weight to one hip and aimed an arrogant fount of spittle into the baked dirt. 'Say that again,' he clipped, narrowing his eyes on the surrounding shadows and clutter.

The sheriff licked his lips and backed instinctively deeper into his cover.

Sol tightened his concentration.

'Tell you somethin',' the older side-kick continued, 'Boyd Knapp ain't goin' to be usin' that blade of his in some while. Mebbe never. Hell, did you see the state of his hand back there? Looked like somethin' a dog had thrown up.' The man winced. 'He needs to see a Doc with a hand like that.'

'Frank won't take no chances brin-gin' a physic into town — not 'til it's vital, and it ain't right now. Boyd'll have to cope.' The lean man spat again. 'Same can't be said for Hal. He didn't stand no chance.'

'Drowned in a dirt-street water trough!' grimaced the thick-set man. 'Would you figure for that? Stickin' it right in Frank's face. I tell you, somethin' ain't natural about this place. There's somebody here — and I ain't for makin' his acquaintance. Nossir!'

The man kicked dirt.

The spitting sidekick's gaze roved like a rattler's search for its supper.

Sheriff Palmer stared vacantly into space as he took in the words, his mind already spinning with images of McCreedy.

Sol Gibbs was almost unaware of the deepening numbness in his knees.

'So who did for Boyd's hand and drowned Hal?' asked the leaning man, pushing irritably at the tightness of his hat. 'You got any notion?'

Another long fount of spittle hit the dirt. 'Same fella as did for Charlie and took the woman back at the Pass. Gotta be.'

'So who in tarnation is he, f'crissake?'

The lean man swung his weight to his other hip. 'Now that, my friend, is somethin' Frank's goin' to be one heap grateful to know.' He grinned. 'What say we oblige?'

'You mean go find the sonofabitch? Here, in this hole of a town?'

'I mean just that,' said the sidekick, easing his hands from his pockets. 'Figure it: f'get them town folk who've pulled out to hole up God knows where. We ain't fussed with them. They ain't nothin'. But the fella who shot Charlie and did his worst through the night is somethin' else. He ain't one of them. Nothin' like.'

'So that much I go along with,' agreed his partner. 'You're right, but how do you know he's still here? You reckon it's likely he's just hidin' out some place? Hell of a risk, ain't it? Damnit, there's enough of us here to flush weevils out of biscuits. I figure he's mebbe pulled out for now. Could be in any one of them creek beds down the trail.'

'That's figurin' the obvious,' said the younger man, cracking his knuckles. 'But this fella ain't obvious. He don't think obvious, and he don't do the obvious.' He cracked a knuckle defiantly. 'He's here. I can feel him.'

The sidekick strolled casually to within a few yards of where the sheriff crouched hidden in the shadows.

'Let's go take a look,' said the man, staring into the distance. 'Startin' with the gospel-sharp's squat back of the church. Likely place for a killer to seek his sanctuary, ain't it?'

★　★　★

'What you reckon?' wheezed Sol Gibbs, dropping to one knee at the sheriff's side. 'You figure for McCreedy bein' here?'

Palmer wiped a dusty hand over the sweat on his face. 'Judgin' by what we've just heard, I'd say McCreedy's been *very* busy! Hell, what's the fella thinkin' of? He goin' to take on Drayton's boys single-handed?'

He grunted irritably. 'He's gotten lucky so far, but when these rats are sobered up and wide awake, who's to say where it'll end? Why didn't the fella . . . ' Palmer's thoughts were stifled in the sudden reality of where he was. 'This ain't no place for us, Sol. Time we shifted.'

'Preacher Peabody's place?' asked the deputy.

'And fast! The two we've just been listenin' to are in one helluva mood for provin' a point to their boss. If McCreedy has headed for the Peabody home, he's goin' to need all the help he can get.'

The two men waited only seconds for the silence to settle again before slipping away to the next sprawl of shadows.

16

The afternoon sun was lower in a clouding sky by the time Sheriff Palmer and Deputy Sol Gibbs had worked their way as close to the Peabody place as they considered safe.

'We'll hold it here at the church and just watch awhile,' said Palmer, hugging the shade of a wall by the spread of one of the few trees still surviving the Peppersville heat and dirt. 'Can't see nothin' of them scumbags yet. Where the hell they disappeared to?'

Sol laid a hand on the sheriff's arm. 'A touch to the left there, side of that old shack. Somethin' movin'.'

Palmer squinted. 'Somethin' movin' sure enough, but it ain't our scumbags.'

Sol eased away to the bulk of the tree's trunk. 'You're right. That's a fella on his own. McCreedy?'

The sheriff merely grunted and

wiped the sweat from his brow. 'Just wait,' he hissed. 'Don't go makin' no hurried moves.'

'Mebbe he's seen us.'

'Yeah, and mebbe Drayton's boys have also seen him.'

They settled to wait, the sheriff stifling his winces at the still throbbing pain of his wound, Sol Gibbs with his gaze fixed like a beam on the shack and the shadows surrounding it.

It was a full three minutes before Sol ventured to speak again. 'This is gettin' spooky,' he murmured, slapping a hand to his neck on the buzz of an attacking fly. 'No sign of Drayton's men, nothin' of McCreedy. Who's watchin' who, f'crissake?' He blinked. 'Mebbe we should try crossin' to the preacher's house. Go take a close look for ourselves. You want I should try? You could cover me easy from here.'

'Sure — and be handy for scrapin' you up when you're dead!' quipped Palmer, shifting his weight. 'I'd guess for McCreedy bein' in that shack out there. But as for the gunslingers — '

They heard the click of the gun hammers before they had drawn another breath.

'Well, now,' seethed a voice that seemed shrouded in steam, 'ain't we just got ourselves somethin' here. A whole sonofabitch lawman and some scumbag I'd reckon for his deputy.' The voice dropped a tone to a growl. 'Don't so much as shift a finger, either of you.'

Palmer stiffened and stifled a wince. Sol Gibbs twitched his shoulders more in anger than irritation. How come they had not heard the gunslingers approaching, he wondered, and what now of the man in the shadows at the shack?

The leaner, spitting gunslinger moved slowly round to face them. 'You fellas have been busy,' he grinned wetly. 'You messed up my good friend Boyd, then did for poor old Hal out there in the street . . . hell, there's gotta be one almighty price on your heads by now. I'll say. So we'll do this nice and easy, eh? We're goin' to take you to meet a certain Mr Frank Drayton who is kinda anxious to make your acquaintance.'

'You hold up some, mister,' snapped Palmer, his face glowing under a lathering of sweat. 'I'm the law in this town, and you'd best not forget it. This is my town, you hear, *my* town? And I'll tell you right now, you and Mr Frank Drayton, that I've got every intention of seein' it restored to them who rightly own it. As for your so-called friends — dead or alive I ain't never set eyes on them. Same goes for my deputy here. So if you're — '

The gunslinger whipped his empty hand across the sheriff's mouth. 'For somebody in your position, you've sure got one hell of a lip on you.'

Palmer gritted his teeth and wiped a trickle of blood from the corner of his mouth. Sol Gibbs clenched his fists.

'Let's shift the pair of 'em,' sneered the gunslinger's partner. 'I wanna hear just how Frank's goin' to deal with a couple of two-bits murderin' scumbags.

Should be music to the ears!'

The sheriff risked no more than a glance back to the shadows at the shack as the gunslingers prodded him away towards the saloon.

The place had looked deserted.

★ ★ ★

'Somethin's gone wrong. And I mean wrong!' Byron Byam looked anxiously round the cluttered wagons and gathered townsfolk to be certain he had not been overheard. 'It don't make no sense,' he went on in a low voice to his audience of Clyde Harte and Ephraim Judd. 'Sheriff and Sol have been gone hours. They should've been here long back. So what's happened, and just where in tarnation is McCreedy?'

'Now hang on there,' soothed Judd, 'we can't have no notion of what's goin' on back in town, or what state it's in. Anythin' could've happened. Mebbe they've met up with McCreedy. Who's to say? Or mebbe they're workin' on some plan in the light of what they've seen. Or mebbe — and here's a thought for you — mebbe the mysterious M.S. has turned up.'

'Yeah, and mebbe the moon's made of cheese!' scoffed Harte from behind a billowing cloud of cigar smoke. 'Hell, I reckon for Byron bein' right here: somethin' has gone wrong; Palmer and Sol should've been back by now, and I for one don't like the look or smell of it.'

'So what you suggestin'?' asked the undertaker.

'I ain't rightly sure what I'm suggestin',' said Harte, lowering his voice secretively. 'All I'm sayin' is, somethin's wrong, just like Byron says, and we shouldn't be for buryin' our heads against the possibility.' He blew smoke. 'And what we mustn't do is get these folk here any more concerned than they already are.'

'I'll go along with that,' agreed Judd. 'Meantime — '

'Meantime, one of us is goin' to have

to ride into town,' clipped Byam. 'And soon. We've got to find out what's happened. We need to know what Drayton's doin', what he's thinkin' — '

'Whoa there!' urged Harte, wafting aside the drifting cigar smoke. 'We're mebbe goin' to have some answers a whole sight sooner than we figured for. Look what's ridin' in.'

The three men swung their gazes to the track leading from the main trail where a lone rider was moving watchfully towards the wagons, a makeshift flag of truce held tight in his left hand.

*   *   *

'Don't nobody make a move,' ordered Doc Walker, threading his way through the gathered townsfolk to Byam's side. 'Let's hear what the man has to say.'

'One of the Drayton gang,' murmured Harte, his interest in the cigar drifting on the wisps of smoke. 'How the hell did he find us?'

'Don't take no figurin', does it?'

muttered the undertaker. 'They've made the sheriff or Sol tell 'em what we did.' He scowled as he polished the lens of his dusty pince-nez.

The Doc took a few steps forward. 'That'll be far enough, mister,' he called. 'Just get to it and say your piece.'

The rider reined his mount to a halt and relaxed, the sweat beading and glistening on his unshaven face. 'Frank Drayton sent me,' he began, his gaze roving smoothly over the faces watching him. 'We've taken the town,' he added with the inkling of a cynical grin.

'That much we've gathered,' snapped Doc. 'You ain't here for the scenery, fella, so what's the deal?'

'Simple enough,' said the man. 'We've a couple of your townsfolk — the sheriff and his deputy — and they've been a whole lot talkative since they made the acquaintance of the boss, if you get my meanin'.'

Doc seethed quietly. Byam ground his teeth. The undertaker's scowl deepened. Harte heeled the half smoked cigar.

'If anythin' happens to Sheriff Palmer — ' began Doc.

'Don't worry, there ain't nothin' goin' to happen to either of 'em, not if you play it smart.' The man shifted to the roll of the mount's flanks. 'Boss says he'll guarantee the safety of your men in return for the women you've got here. You send them saloon gals into town, and we'll release the sheriff. Boss reckons it a fair exchange.' The man's gaze narrowed to a darker stare. 'You've got 'til sundown.'

'And if we don't go along with Drayton?' asked Doc.

The man shrugged. 'Wouldn't care to say, but seein' as how the fellas concerned ain't exactly figurin' high in the boss's estimation right now, I'd reckon them for coffins — eventually.'

The townsfolk murmured anxiously among themselves. A woman gasped and stifled a sob. 'Sonofabitch,' hissed Judd. Byam twitched under a sudden chill. Harte sweated.

'Choice is yours,' said the rider, taking a firmer hold of the reins. 'But just remember: you've got 'til sundown. We'll be waitin'.'

17

'Impossible! Out of the question. Can't be done and won't be done, not while I'm still drawin' breath.' Clyde Harte's sweat-soaked face disappeared like a balloon behind a swirl of cigar smoke. 'It's tough, I know, but that's that. My gals ain't goin' nowhere, not no how, not under any circumstances,' he added on a wheeze.

Byron Byam turned from a group of townsmen gathered at the side of a wagon. 'All very well talkin' like that standin' here, but imagine how Palmer's feelin', the thoughts goin' through Sol's head. Hell, they'll know the deal, they'll know the stakes. How in heck are they goin' to see things?'

'Byron's right,' said a man at the front of the gathering, 'but I don't reckon for there bein' a man here who'd go along with the likes of Sheri and her girls bein' traded for the sheriff's life. I'd reckon for Palmer and Sol bein' willin' to die than stand witness to that.'

There were murmurings of agreement among the town men.

'So we let them die,' said Judd bluntly, polishing his pince-nez. 'Just like that. Ignore the deal, leave the sheriff and Sol to their miserable fate and stay right where we are.' He fixed the spectacles dramatically and peered over the tops of the glinting lens. 'Then what?' he asked solemnly. 'What do we do when Frank Drayton and his boys have gone about their murderous business?'

There were long moments of a deep silence when nothing stirred and hardly a soul seemed to breathe.

'That's the real problem, ain't it?' said Doc carefully as he left the wagon where Preacher Peabody was being tended. 'What do we do when Palmer and Sol Gibbs are dead?' He gazed round the watching faces. 'Can't speak for what will happen to us, but I can sure as sunup tell you what Frank Drayton will do. He'll still want the women. 'Course he will, because that's the only luxury he ain't got in Peppersville; the one thing his boys will be wantin' once the novelty of free booze and food begins to pale.' He paused. 'Don't doubt it, he'll be back to help himself. He knows where we are and we ain't got no place to run to from here.'

'Then we'd best get ourselves organized and ride into town,' croaked a man, pushing himself clear of his wagon. 'If Drayton's boys hit us here, they'll take everythin'. And I got a wife and daughters to look to. I say we ride.'

Another murmur of agreement swept through the gathering.

'What about that fella, McCreedy?' piped the old-timer.

'What about him?' echoed a man in the shadows. 'We ain't seen nor heard nothin' of him. He's pulled out. Figured he would anyhow.'

'Can't say that for certain,' snapped Byam, adjusting his coat. 'Damnit, we just don't know. Anythin' could have happened. Fella might be anywhere. Who's to say? Who's to know?'

'I know one thing for sure,' snapped Sheri Ward, bustling her way to Doc Walker's side, a flushed look of determination on her face. 'I know we're wastin' time. I know sundown's fast approaching, and I know only too well that Sheriff Palmer and Sol Gibbs are within a couple of hours of losing their lives if we don't do something. So we will.'

She swung round to stare directly into Old Stoney's eyes. 'Hitch a wagon, fast as you can. Me and the girls are going to town!'

★　★　★

Frank Drayton watched the shapes moving through the haze of stale smoke as if counting ghosts.

Boyd Knapp, his knife hand swathed

in a mound of bandages, paced the saloon bar like a caged tiger in pain. Somebody should go help him, he thought, get him drunk enough to sleep out the agony of his wound.

Myers Forman was fidgeting; he was always fidgeting, getting jumpy at the slightest sound, the merest hint of something out of the normal. He was getting old, too old for this game. One of these days somebody would do something about him.

Drayton's gaze settled on another ghost: Sheriff Palmer, lawman hereabouts and doubtless a decent fellow behind the badge he wore. It would be a pity to have to kill him. But he would, and personally too, when the time came. There could be no half measures where lawmen were concerned. Same would go for his scowling deputy.

Question was: had these two really been responsible for reducing Knapp to a whining dog, for drowning Hal in the town's street water trough, or had there been a third party involved? The

162

gunman who had taken out Charlie at the shack? And if there had been a third man, then where was he now?

The sheriff and his deputy had been quickly 'persuaded' to reveal the whereabouts of the townfolk, but offered nothing by way of so much as a hint of an accomplice.

Drayton grunted to himself and drummed his fingers on the drink-stained table, his thoughts moving beyond the ghosts, the smoke haze, the foul smelling bar to somewhere far . . .

'What yuh reckon, Frank, we goin' to get them girls?' clipped Forman, tapping the toe of his boot on the floorboards. 'Boys are gettin' restless.'

Drayton's eyes opened wide on the haze and gloom. 'Message has been delivered. Them town-folk know the deal. Plain enough. So now we wait. 'T'ain't sundown yet.'

Forman turned his attention to the sheriff roped tight to a chair in a corner. 'What you reckon, lawman? You figure for them folk out there givin' up the gals?'

Palmer stayed silent, conscious of Sol Gibbs, similarly roped to a chair at his side, seething quietly.

'Ain't sayin', eh?' grinned Forman. 'Well, it don't matter none either way in your case, does it, seein' as how you won't be partakin' of what's on offer!'

'To hell with you,' mumbled Sol.

'Sure, sure,' said Forman, the grin spreading to a smile. 'Well, you just save your breath, fella. You mebbe ain't got that many left. Don't want to waste any, do you?'

Drayton shifted impatiently, his fingers flattening on the table. 'Go take a look around town, Myers. See what's happenin'.'

Forman scuffed the boot across the floor. 'Can tell you exactly what's goin' on out there, Frank,' he mouthed. 'Do it with my eyes closed, so to speak. Boys'll be gathered in the street, all with their faces turned like moons to the main trail . . . just waitin', quiet as mice, not sayin' a word . . . waitin' on the sight of a wagonload of women. That's what's happenin' out there.'

'Go take a look anyway,' ordered Drayton. 'Now, f'crissake!'

'You got it Frank,' soothed Forman, backing to the batwings. 'Just like you say.'

Boyd Knapp paced out of the shadows, his bandaged hand cradled in his arm. 'That fella's beginnin' to get up my nose,' he croaked, staring into the darkening street. 'Sooner we torch this town and ride out the better. Place is like a plague.'

Somebody would have to do something about Knapp, thought Drayton, watching the ghosts again.

★ ★ ★

Sheriff Palmer listened again for the sound of what he was sure had been a movement somewhere at the rear of the saloon, perhaps in Clyde Harte's private quarters, or maybe in the storeroom. A sound, he thought, that might very well have been a presence. McCreedy? Wishful thinking. Clutching at straws. It could just as easily have been one of Drayton's sidekicks scuffing through his search for a fresh bottle. Or a scavenging dog left behind in the exodus. Anything. Anyone. He squirmed against the tightness of the ropes binding him to the chair, tried to flex his fingers, winced at the throb of his still troublesome hand, and glanced sideways at his deputy.

Sol had been struggling for close on an hour to weaken the rope at his wrists.

'Any luck?' hissed Palmer.

'Too darned slow,' muttered Sol. 'But I ain't givin' up. Not yet, damnit.' The sweat beaded on his brow. 'What about the girls? You figure for them ridin' in?'

Palmer sighed. 'They'll argue for and against for a while, weighin' this, weighin' that, some for, some against, but I'd bet on Sheri bein' for it. She'll bring the girls in. She'll see it as buyin' us some time.'

'But will it?' asked Sol.

'Mebbe. Mebbe not. Depends.'

'If you're still reckonin' on that fella, McCreedy — '

'I ain't,' hissed Palmer. 'And keep your voice down.' He glanced quickly at the apparently dozing Drayton at the table, the restlessly pacing Boyd Knapp. 'But somebody did for that fella there, and put the water trough to good use. And he weren't no ghost!'

'Even so — '

'You two all through with the yappin'?' snapped Knapp, his eyes flashing angrily in his drawn, pain-racked face. 'So what you got to yap about, f'crissake? Not a deal by my reckonin'. So shut it, eh? I ain't for havin' so much damned noise around me.' He paced to the batwings. 'Town's full of noise. Everybody yappin' and shoutin' — '

Knapp's droning voice was drowned in the sudden cheers and whoops from the street as the sidekicks greeted the approach of a wagon heading down the trail.

'If that's who I think it is . . . ' murmured Sol.

Sheriff Palmer swallowed. Boyd Knapp cradled his shattered hand and seethed quietly between clenched teeth.

Drayton blinked on the smoke haze, came slowly to his feet and crossed to the batwings, wondering if Myers Forman had done as he had ordered.

18

'This is far enough,' said Doc Walker, reining his mount to the deeper shadows at a rocky outcrop just short of town. 'Any closer and we might be spotted.'

He waited for Byron Byam to join him, settle his horse at his side and tighten his gaze on the sprawl of the silhouetted shapes some distance away.

'Only one light out there as I can see,' murmured the storekeeper. 'Seems like Drayton's made the saloon his headquarters. Now there's a surprise!' He ran a nervous finger round his collar. 'Shudder to think what state the store's in. Hell, don't bear thinkin' about.'

'Then don't,' clipped Doc. 'Think about Sheri and the girls. Wouldn't give a deal right now for their prospects through the next few hours.'

'Can't just leave 'em like that, can we? Shadowed them this far, but now what? Do we sit here, high-tail it back to the wagons, or mebbe we should get to strikin' some sort of deal with Drayton?'

'And you'd rate a scumbag of his type holdin' to his word?' said Doc, narrowing his gaze on the silhouetted buildings of the town, the empty street, the lone light breaking through the gathering dust like a yellow eye. 'No deal with Drayton would be worth the breath of sayin' it. He'd renege on his own mother if he saw a dollar in it for him.'

Byam grunted and patted his restive mount's neck. 'Meantime, there's Preacher Peabody crippled for life, there's Sheriff Palmer and Sol Gibbs out there in Drayton's hands, and now, damn it, we've just made a gift of Sheri and the girls. So what, in the name of sanity, is left?'

'There's McCreedy and whoever his mysterious friend M.S. happens to be.'

170

'And you'd rate the gun-totin' teacher as bein' our best bet — our only bet — along with a body we ain't never seen, who might not even exist, and even if he does, ain't under no obligation to come ridin' to the rescue of Peppersville? I tell you straight, Doc — '

'Easy,' warned Doc, pointing ahead, 'somethin's happenin' up there.'

The two men narrowed their gazes and concentrated on what they could make out of the sudden gathering of gunslingers outside the Broken Nugget saloon.

'Seems like they're inspectin' somethin',' murmured Byam.

'Can't see what,' said Doc, easing forward in the saddle. 'Gettin' too dark to make out much of anythin'.'

'Mebbe we could get closer. Perhaps if we . . . Hold it! What's that?'

Doc urged his mount a step forward. 'A rider. Fella alone. Damn it, if that ain't . . . Too damned right, that's McCreedy comin' this way.'

'How the hell did he find us? What's he want?'

'Sit tight, my friend, and we might find out.'

★ ★ ★

Frank Drayton walked through a slow, measured circle, the steps firm, the pace thoughtful, hands in a tight grip behind him, his gaze fixed and unblinking on the objects arranged neatly in the pool of light on the boardwalk.

The men watching him remained silent, pale, blank looks of disbelief and fear filling their faces. One man, his mouth thick with a wad of chewing tobacco, wiped a dribble of spittle from his lips, then spat violently into the street. ' 'T'ain't natural,' he muttered, his voice grating like a serrated edge drawn across rock.

'Say that again,' murmured another. 'I'm tellin' you, the place is haunted.'

'Cut that talk,' said Knapp from the shadows, the pain in his hand forgotten for the moment.

'Easy to say,' protested a lean, unwashed sidekick, his broken teeth gleaming in the lantern glow, 'but how'd yuh explain this?' He gestured to the pool of light. 'Myers Forman's hat, his pants and boots — and no sign of his body. Explain that!'

'I can't, not yet,' said Knapp above the mutterings of the others. 'But there is an explanation, got to be.'

'Tell me again,' croaked Drayton, coming to a halt with his back to the batwings. 'Who found these?'

'I did,' piped a short, stocky man with a hooded left eye and scarred face. 'Back of the mercantile. I was along with the boys in the street here waitin' on them gals arrivin'. Got to thinkin' it was time I had a clean shirt, so I went to the store's back door figurin' on helpin' myself, and there they were — hat, pants, boots, just left in the dirt, almost like I was supposed to find them. Spooked me somethin' rotten, don't mind tellin' yuh. But there weren't nothin' of Myers. Not a hair of him.'

'So what's happened to him?' grunted a man at the fellow's shoulder.

'Well, don't just stand there like dead whiskers in a barber's bowl, go and find him,' growled Drayton, his gaze flaring. 'You keep your hands off them girls 'til Myers is found, you hear me? No Myers, no girls. Now get to it.'

The sidekicks muttered and mumbled among themselves as they filed away to the dark street.

'I want every last inch of this two-bits town scoured like you were cleanin' a bone,' Drayton called after them. 'Every last corner. Every speck of dirt. Take the place apart if you have to.'

He watched until the men had disappeared into the darkness, then turned to Boyd Knapp. 'Go and help yourself to one of them gals — if you're able,' he mocked.

'You figurin' what I'm figurin'?' said Knapp, cradling his hand again. 'I reckon you are. I reckon you think whoever shot Charlie is right here in Peppersville. Right now, even as we speak. And you know somethin' — he's winnin'? He's got us right where he wants us.' He relaxed his weight to one hip. 'I don't figure for us havin' much time for girls, do you? I reckon we've already got our hands full, so to speak.'

★   ★   ★

It was a little after half past nine by the clock on the saloon bar wall when they found the body of Myers Forman.

The gunslinger, a close partner of long-standing to the Drayton brothers, had been hanged from the loading beam at the rear of the livery stables above the manure heap, his stockinged feet scraping the surface of the last shovelled level, his clothing and flesh reeking of the stench.

He still had the rope at his neck when they carried the body into the bar and laid it within sight of Frank Drayton.

'Been dead some time by the feel of him,' said one of the pale-faced sidekicks. 'Somebody must have jumped him.'

'I can see for myself,' growled Drayton, coming slowly to his feet at the table where he had been seated with Sheri Ward at his side. 'I don't need nothin' spellin' out from nobody. You got that? Nothin'. You keep your mouths shut all of you, and you listen. You all listen!'

The nervous gathering of sidekicks grunted and murmured their under-standing. Boyd Knapp licked his lips, but stifled a cynical grin.

Sheri Ward stiffened, glanced anx-iously at the already shivering bar girls and mouthed for them to stay silent. Her gaze moved quickly to the still-roped sheriff and his deputy. They looked close to being all in, she thought, but the sight of Forman's body had sparked a new life in their eyes, as if in some way bringing a message to them. McCreedy, she wondered, risking

176

a soft smile in response to Palmer's sudden wink. Was the man here? Had he been responsible for the death of Forman?

She stiffened again as Frank Drayton grasped the neck of a half-empty bottle of whiskey, moved unsteadily to the bar and stood with his back to it, his glare through the lantern lit gloom like a hot coal in a hole.

'This is enough,' he began. 'I ain't takin' no more. Same goes for you fellas. You agreed on that? Enough's enough. Ain't nobody on this godforsaken earth does for our good friend like this and gets away with it. No how. Nossir! What you say?'

The sidekicks murmured and nodded.

'It's like you put it, Frank,' said a man at the batwings. 'Enough's enough. We're with you.'

'Good,' smiled Drayton. 'Never doubted it.' He gulped noisily from the bottle. 'So here's what we do.' The bottle thudded to the bar. The glare gleamed. The lips tightened. 'We're goin' to scrub this town from the map, leave nothin', not a stick, not so much as the smell of the place. Peppersville's goin' to be Leverton all over again — only a hundred times worse!'

The sidekicks whooped, stamped their feet, crashed bottles and glasses to tables, slapped backs and raised defiant fists.

'That's the way of it, Frank,' shouted a man at the window.

'Torch it,' called another. 'Put it to flames!'

'And scatter the ashes!'

Boyd Knapp smiled as he cradled his crushed hand. Sheri Ward and the bar girls shivered. Sheriff Palmer moaned inwardly. Sol Gibbs seethed and strained against the ropes at his wrists.

Drayton raised his arms. 'I hear you, boys, loud and clear,' he grinned. 'And don't you fret none, we're goin' to do just as you say down to the very last flame. But meantime . . . ' He paused a moment. 'Yeah, meantime we've got things to do. Important things.'

The sidekicks fell silent. Drayton gulped from the bottle again and rolled a glassy gaze over the watching faces.

'So what you got in mind, Frank?' asked a man at the front of the group.

'Simple,' announced Drayton, replacing the bottle as he stood to his full height. 'Anythin' you fellas want or take a fancy to is yours. If this town's got it, help yourselves. And that includes the girls here.' He stared at the clock on the wall. 'You've got the hours of darkness. We strike at first light, and Peppersville will be no more by noon.'

'What about the lawman and his deputy?' asked a man lounging at the batwings.

Drayton stared at the two roped men and grinned. 'They can start countin' the hours til we burn 'em — alive!'

19

Doc Walker watched intently as Old Stoney checked out the line of loose-hitched mounts.

'How many we got ridin'?' asked Byron Byam at his shoulder.

Doc broke his concentration and gazed over the moonlit night. 'Twenty will saddle up,' he said quietly. 'They're the best and the fittest. Got to leave some here, o'course, to look to the women and young 'uns.'

'That goin' to be enough?' asked Byam.

'Goin' to have to be. Can't spare more. But you heard what McCreedy said out there when he joined us: if we do it right, follow his orders to the letter and don't lose our heads, we might just pull this off. It's a gamble and, hell, there's enough to go wrong, but it's a throw of the dice. Probably the only one we're goin' to get.'

Byam pulled nervously at the folds of his coat. 'Just hope McCreedy's readin' this right,' he muttered.

'If anybody's readin' it, McCreedy's our man. You saw him, heard what he had to say. He told us what he'd done and what he planned. Couldn't have been plainer.'

'Didn't see a deal of him buried back there in the rocks, but I'll grant you he talked sense. Mebbe we can pull this off, but, damn it, we're trustin' to Drayton doin' exactly as McCreedy's figurin' he will. Supposin' he don't, what then? Supposin' — '

The two men turned at the approach of Clyde Harte through a billowing swirl of cigar smoke. 'I just hope Sheri Ward knew what she was doin',' he muttered, gesturing with the cigar lodged in his stubby fingers. 'Pullin' out like she did . . . all them gals along with her. Hell, it don't bear thinkin' to.'

'Mebbe you're just worryin' about your investment,' quipped Byam with another tug of his coat. 'We've all lost out in this, Clyde. Won't be a business left in town worth the countin' to once Drayton's rats have scavenged it, but that ain't the point. The point is — '

'I'll tell you what the point is,' said Doc, swinging his gaze from Old Stoney and the line-hitched mounts. 'Point is savin' lives and fightin' for our freedom to have a town, whatever state we find it in. We've got Sheri and the girls doin' their best for us out there — and no tellin' at what cost — and Sheriff Palmer and Sol Gibbs ain't exactly whoopin' it up at a hoedown, are they? And that's without mentionin' McCreedy . . . So to hell for now as to who or what he is, let's just get to doin' as he's planned. Every last man of us.'

Old Stoney waved from the line. 'All set, Doc,' he called. 'Fellas can start saddlin' up when they're ready.'

'Right,' said Doc, 'so let's get the men together. Check out the guns, ammunition, canteens. We pull out exactly one hour before first light and wait on McCreedy's orders when we reach the rock cover just short of town. Don't have to tell you that silence is the priority. We ride real easy, steady pace, no talkin', nobody gettin' ahead of the others. And stay close packed. We reach them rocks like shadows.'

'Tall order,' murmured Byam.

'Tall or short, it's the only one we have — and we're stayin' with it.'

Doc turned from the others and moved into the soft glow of the lanterns among the wagons. He acknowledged the anxious faces watching him. They all looked the same, he thought. All uncertain, fearful, waiting on a new day that might never dawn.

He grunted to himself and headed quickly for the preacher's wagon. It was time somebody got to praying.

★　★　★

'You still with me?' hissed Sheriff Palmer, glancing anxiously at the slumped body of Sol Gibbs roped to

183

the chair at his side.

'Concentratin',' murmured the deputy without lifting his chin from his chest. 'Another fifteen minutes and my hands'll be free.' He grunted quietly, disregarding the lines of sweat that dripped from his face.

'Go easy,' urged Palmer. 'We're only goin' to get one crack at this.'

'I know. I hear what's bein' said.' Sol grunted again. 'We'll make it just so long as them scumbags stay occupied.'

'I don't reckon we figure high in their interests right now.' The sheriff turned his gaze slowly round the bar, narrowing his eyes on the blurred shapes of the gunslingers and Sheri Ward's girls, the still-pacing Boyd Knapp, the shadowy presence of Frank Drayton now seated in the darkest corner. 'Everybody's pretty well occupied I'd say,' he added quietly.

Sol Gibbs deepened his concentration. The sheriff continued to watch and wait anxiously. How long did they have, he wondered? Was Drayton serious in his promise to torch the town come first light? Would he really do it? He would, he decided. That was Drayton, and now at his meanest and blackest with the death of Myers Forman haunting him; a killing that had seemed to mock at his hold on the town and authority among his men.

He had glared and stared like a sullen crow through the removal of the body from the bar, the warning clear enough in the unblinking set of his eyes. He would have his boys ransack the town, strip it of anything of value, then simply burn it. Erase it from the map and anyone he chose to burn with it.

But what of McCreedy, pondered Palmer, and Doc Walker, Byam, Judd, the others out at the creek? What were they planning? Could they know of Drayton's intentions? But even if they did . . .

His thoughts were broken at the sound of Drayton's voice.

'Two hours, no more,' he ordered,

glaring round his men in their preoccu-
pations with the girls. 'Then we move.'
He came slowly to his feet, the gaze
shifting to narrow on the sheriff and Sol
Gibbs.

'I'm goin' to give you pesky flies a
chance to save somethin' of your skin,'
he growled when he finally stood over
them, arms folded, face glistening
under a skein of sweat. 'Now I know
there's somebody out there in this
two-bits town of yours who's givin' me
and my boys one whole heap of
unnecessary grief. And that somebody
is carryin' one helluva price on his
head.' He unfolded his arms and
clamped his hands to his waist. 'So, we,
which is to say you and me, get to some
positive dealin', eh?'

'Forget it,' croaked Palmer. 'I'd as
soon deal with a rattler.'

'Big talk, Mr Lawman,' grinned
Drayton, 'but mebbe not so big when
you hear what I got to say.' He gestured
for Boyd Knapp to bring Sheri Ward to
him. 'Now you see here, fella, if you

186

don't get to tellin' me all about the killer out there, this pretty face and body gets to bein' carved up like beef at a cattleman's supper. And when we've done with her, there's always the girls to get to work on, ain't there? After all, we ain't plannin' on leavin' too many breathin' bodies behind when we finally pull out.'

Drayton's grin spread to a wet smile. 'Like I say, we got just two more hours, so I'm all ears, fellas. And Miss Ward here is already beginnin' to sweat.'

★ ★ ★

The band of twenty armed and grimly determined men of Peppersville left their wagons, their women-folk, families and few possessions and rode out of the scrub-darkened creek while the moon was still high and bright and the night skimmed with the softest of white clouds.

The air was still thin and chill when, like ghost riders, they reined into the sprawling rock cover just short of the besieged town.

Doc Walker led the men into the deepest shadows and waited until they were settled before addressing them. 'Don't have to spell out again what we're about,' he said carefully, watching their damp, moonlit faces. 'This is as far as we go for now, temptin' as it is to keep right on ridin' and shoot the hell out of the Drayton mob.'

'You got it, Doc,' piped a man from the darkness. 'I'd sure as damnit do just that. Why, if I had my way — '

'Well, you ain't,' said Doc curtly. 'There ain't none of you havin' a way. There's only one, and that's goin' to be McCreedy's way — which is what we're waitin' on right now. Meantime, we post lookouts, we keep a sharp eye on the town, and we stay silent. I ain't reckonin' on any of them Drayton scum leavin' town. Too darned busy with other things, but we can't take any risks.'

'You bet they're busy,' grunted Clyde

Harte. 'Wreckin' my saloon for one. As for Sheri and the girls . . . hell! Just hope Sheriff Palmer and Sol are still breathin'.'

Doc flicked the reins to his mount through his fingers. 'There's a lot at stake out there for all of us, so there can't be no messin' up. Judgin' by what I seen comin' down the trail, the town seems quiet enough. Dangerously quiet.' He raised a hand for silence. 'Let's post the lookouts, but remember, it's McCreedy we're waitin' on, nobody else.'

'If he's alive,' murmured the store-keeper to the night.

20

The gunslinger's head was already pounding like a roll of thunder when he thudded through the batwings to the boardwalk, reeled drunkenly for his balance and finally made it to the street. He stood swaying for a moment, his glazed eyes rolling into an uncertain focus, then staggered away towards an alley at the side of Byron Byam's dry goods store and general mercantile.

The man had no notion of his direction, where his steps might lead or where, when his sense of staying upright deserted him, he might collapse. He was not much bothered. All he did know in the fuddle of what passed for thoughts was that he needed air and space.

He was getting his fill of both as he staggered from the alley, paused, swayed, blinked on the still moonlit darkness and crossed the open ground fronting the Peppersville community's white-painted clapboard church.

'Lord above, ain't that a sight to behold?' he slurred as he paused again and fixed his swimming gaze on the double doors at the top of a flight of steps. 'Might just have myself a quiet moment there. Sure, and why not? Should've brought a bottle. Yessir. Share and share alike just as the Good Book says. You bet . . . just so long as I get the most, eh? You bet!'

He tittered and staggered on, one hand reaching for the rail at the side of the steps.

The man had taken a grip, steadied his bulk and tottered into an uncertain climb when the door above him opened with an eerily creaking flourish and the space filled with the dark shape of a staring figure.

The gunslinger's eyes were suddenly focused like black stones frozen in snow. He gazed glassily, mouth open, one hand holding to his grip on the rail, the other as dead as a mudpack at the end of a loose, hanging arm.

'Who in the name of hell's-devils are you?' he mouthed, his face lifted to the man's burning stare. 'I heard about you back there,' he mumbled. 'You're the fella . . . ' His voice trailed away on a slur as his free hand moved to the holstered Colt at his waist. 'Yeah, I heard,' he croaked. 'Yuh did for Charlie Drayton, Myers Forman and my good friend, Hal, didn't yuh? I seen what yuh did, mister . . . '

He had drawn the Colt and was levelling it in his grip when the knife blade glinted on the moonlight in its flight from the man's hand to the gunslinger's chest where it buried itself with a thud.

The drunk stood perfectly still for what seemed long seconds through a chilling silence. His eyes did not move, his mouth stayed open, the Colt hung impotent in his grip. Then, as if moving through slow motion, he fell back, hit the dirt and did not move again.

The dark figure in the doorway continued to stare for a moment before stepping back, closing the doors as he went to leave only the darkness to cover the body of the gunslinger.

Five minutes later the Peppersville community church bell began to toll its mournful message of a death that night.

★　★　★

The silence fell across the saloon bar of the Broken Nugget like a deadly breath that dulled and numbed.

'Yuh hear that?' croaked a suddenly shaking man at the batwings, his flat, fearful gaze turned to the street and the echoing toll of the bell. 'F'crissake, do yuh hear that — any of yuh?' The man turned to the smoke-filled, liquor-hazed bar. 'I ain't dreamin' this, not no how I ain't.'

'You ain't dreamin',' murmured Boyd Knapp, cradling his shattered hand as he moved like a shadow to the batwings.

'And neither am I,' croaked a barrel-belly man, pushing a half-naked bar girl from his lap. 'I know what that means.'

'Me too,' groaned a gunslinger hitching his trousers to his waist.

'Another body?' echoed a man at a window.

'Slicky Brown said as how he needed some air a while back,' piped a voice from somewhere under the stairs to the balcony.

'I heard him say that,' followed a man shadowing Knapp at the batwings. 'Perhaps we should go take a look.'

'No,' snapped Knapp, glancing quickly at the sheriff and Sol Gibbs roped to their chairs. 'Somebody go rouse Frank from that back room, then untie the lawman. If anybody's headin' into that street, he ain't goin' without a shield.' The gunslinger grinned. 'Let's see if the fella out there is as keen on killin' when there's a sheriff with a barrel at his head to be reckoned with.'

Doc Walker listened carefully to the final fading toll of the church bell then, as the silence thickened again, turned with a soft smile on his worn face to Byron Byam at his side. 'Well, you couldn't ask for clearer proof than that. McCreedy's alive and, by my figurin', keepin' busy!'

'You think we should move?' asked Harte anxiously.

'I say not,' said the undertaker polishing his pince-nez. 'Leastways not yet. Mebbe McCreedy'll turn up here. Mebbe he'll get a message to us. Either way, I say we sit tight now 'til first light.'

The townsmen murmured quietly among themselves.

'We could go high-tailin' into town and make things worse for somebody — Sheriff Palmer, Sol Gibbs, Sheri and the gals,' counselled a man among the gathering. 'We sure as hell don't want to go doin' that.'

'You're right, fella,' agreed Byam

nodding his head. 'McCreedy's workin' alone at the moment. We could get to foulin' that up.'

'And don't let's overlook Drayton,' sweated Harte, dabbing at his neck with a bandanna. 'No sayin' to his next move, is there?'

'I can guess,' said Old Stoney, rolling his shirt-sleeves over his massive arms. 'His patience will get to wearin' thin as a twig. Then it'll snap, and, zap, that'll be the end of Peppersville.' He settled his hands on his hips. 'Damned if we make a move; damned if we don't make it in time.'

The townsmen fell silent again.

'There'll be the first hint of light in an hour,' murmured Doc, scanning the still, velvet night sky. 'Unless things happen otherwise, we wait 'til then. Minute we see the light, we make our move. No more debatin', no goin' back.' He consulted his timepiece in the palm of his hand. 'Sixty minutes exactly.'

★ ★ ★

Sheriff Palmer squirmed, swore through clenched teeth and glowered like a sore-headed bull as the sidekick twisted his arm tighter into his back and marched him across the crowded saloon bar to the batwings.

'If you're thinkin' for one minute — ' began Palmer.

'Don't tell me what to think or do,' growled Frank Drayton, wiping the back of his hand across his lips. 'I'm callin' all the shots here, mister, and that includes the one that'll do for you when I'm good and ready.'

He turned his narrowed eyes to the boardwalk and the still-dark street beyond the 'wings and let his gaze probe among the shapes and shadows. Who was it out there? Where was he hiding? Was he still in the church with the body of Slicky Brown at his feet? Hell, did the fellow really think he could take on the Drayton gang single-handed? Was he that dumb?

'What's his name?' asked Drayton, flicking his gaze to Palmer in the sidekick's grip. 'And don't give me no lip. Fella ain't got long to live, anyhow. Just like to give him a handle. So what's his name?'

'Last time I heard it was McCreedy — and you'd better note it well,' scowled the sheriff. 'You're goin' to be hearin' one helluva lot more of it before another day's done.'

Drayton grunted and turned to Boyd Knapp. 'We know a McCreedy from any place?' he asked.

Knapp shrugged and cradled his crushed hand. 'Don't mean nothin' to me. Only scumbag I keep tabs on is Matt Stewart, and I ain't heard nothin' of him since North Rocks.'

Palmer stiffened at the mention of North Rocks, his mind reeling back to the wire McCreedy had received from M.S. He swallowed. Could M.S. be Matt Stewart? If Boyd and Drayton knew of the man, could it also be —

'Who gives a damn, anyhow,' growled

Drayton. 'Fella's just a two-bits sonofa-bitch who fancies his chances as some big noise. Well, if this McCreedy's taken out Slicky Brown it's time to teach him a lesson, then we get to dealin' with this town once and for all.'

Drayton swung round to face Palmer, stepping to within only inches of the lawman's sweating face. 'All I've had out of you so far is a name,' he sneered through a liquor-laced breath. 'And you've gotten lucky where the woman is concerned, but time's movin' on now and we got things to attend to — not least this stinkin' town of yours. So you want my advice, mister, you do exactly as I say. And I mean exactly.' He flashed a glance at the sidekick. 'Get him out there. You know what to do.'

They pushed, kicked, heaved the sheriff from the saloon to the street, the sidekick holding him flanked now by a half-dozen more. The men moved on until they had reached beyond the shadows to where the early dawn light was making its first slow creep through breaking cloud, then halted, the barrel of a Colt pressed tight into Palmer's temple.

'Listen up there, mister, wherever you are,' shouted one of the sidekicks into echoing space. 'We got a message for you from Frank Drayton. You hearin' this? A message from the man himself, and it's simple enough. You've got just thirty minutes to be out of this town and on your way. If you happen to be fool enough to stay, the sheriff here will be the first to die. Then it'll be the turn of his deputy, and then . . . well, now, we might get to takin' our time with the killin' of them girls we're holdin' back there.'

Sheriff Palmer squirmed, but only to feel the bite of a boot in his leg, a tighter twist of the arm pinned in his back, the pressure of the barrel at his temple.

'You got the message, fella?' called the sidekick. 'You understand? You'd better.' He turned to the thick-set man at his side. 'Go see what you can find of

Slicky at the church. And watch yourself. The boss ain't for losin' no more men.'

Palmer squirmed again as the party backed from the street to the bar, the sweat lathering across his shoulders, the dawn air chilling its sting. It would be full light to day soon enough.

But how much of it was he going to see?

21

Two men were carrying the body of Slicky Brown to the boardwalk fronting the Broken Nugget when the shot rang out from high among the rooftops on the opposite side of the street. The man supporting Slicky's legs was killed instantly.

Minutes later there were two dead bodies spreading early morning shadows across the dirt, and a bar crowded with men struck suddenly dumb, their empty gazes staring into nowhere.

Only the remorseless tick of the clock disturbed the heavy silence until, with a thud as his boot hit the wall in anger, a man at the window spat and cursed. 'Sonofabitch!' he growled. 'I say we kill the lawman now. Him and his deputy. Shoot 'em in the head and toss their bodies to the buzzards. Show this McCreedy rat we mean business.'

'Nobody messes with us like this,' croaked another man. 'So what we waitin' on, Frank?'

Drayton drummed his fingers on the bar, flicked at an empty glass, glared into the stained surface as if seeing himself in a mirror, and grunted. 'We ain't waitin' on nothin',' he said, conscious of the twitching nerve in his cheek. 'We don't never wait on nothin' and not nobody, not even Peppersville, specially not Peppersville.'

The sidekicks gathered in the gloomy, smoke-veiled saloon murmured their approval.

'That's sayin' it straight,' grinned a sidekick, slapping a bar girl's buttocks. 'Yuh hear that, gal, we don't wait on nothin' and nobody. Nossir! Give us the word, boss.'

'I'm all through with this town,' piped the man at the window. 'Ain't we all? Don't that go for most of us?'

There were calls of agreement, a stamping of boots, thudding of bottles to tables.

'This town owes us,' called a youth, lifting a half-empty bottle of whiskey to his mouth. 'It's taken some of our best, so let's get to the torchin' and toss McCreedy right in the heat of it.' He gulped at the bottle, then threw it aside with a curse. 'We're sure as hell waitin' now, Frank — waitin' on your word.'

Drayton's gaze shifted quickly from Boyd Knapp to Sheriff Palmer, Sol Gibbs, Sheri Ward and the scattering of dishevelled girls. 'You got it,' he hissed. 'Go to it, and don't leave nothin' standin'!'

*   *   *

Boots scuffed and thudded across the floorboards; men buckled gunbelts into place, checked out their weapons, holstered Colts with an ominous grunt of satisfaction, settled their hats, hitched their pants and slapped the girls. Some went in search of more whiskey, others lit cheroots, one man took the pendant from a girl's neck, clenched it in the palm of his hand, then pocketed it. Another strolled to the batwings and simply stared, silent and alone, into the empty street where the first morning light was spreading like slow water.

Sheriff Palmer, standing free now at Frank Drayton's side but under the watchful eyes of Boyd Knapp, glanced anxiously at Sol Gibbs, wondering if he had finally succeeded in freeing his hands and, if he had, when he might make a move. Not yet, he hoped. Not until the sidekicks had left the bar and gone about their grisly business.

Sheri Ward began to gather her girls to her like a mother hen clucking over her chicks. Drayton poured himself a long measure from a fresh bottle. Knapp cradled his hand, winced and cursed in the same breath.

The sidekicks began to gather at the 'wings. Eyes watched. Voices came and went, some confident, others less so.

'Street's quiet enough now.'

'That's 'cus that sonofabitch ain't got a target.'

'Let's give him one, f'crissake! A dozen and more guns against one — what chance has he got?'

'Them bodies are still out there. Somebody should shift 'em.'

'You volunteerin'?'

'Let's cut the talk and go finish it.'

The sidekicks tightened on the batwings, their gazes cautious as they moved silently to the boardwalk, hands hovering over holstered guns. They grouped like a flock of uncertain birds awaiting the signal to migrate. Three men strayed to the street, looked around them, to left and right, scanned the empty rooftops, darker doorways and windows.

'Fella's not for makin' himself known,' called one, gesturing an arm across the deserted street.

The men eased clear of the shadows, still watchful but beginning now to find their confidence.

'Never did like this dump of a town,'

growled an older man. 'Be glad to see the back of it.'

'So get to it,' snapped Knapp from the boardwalk. 'Start with that sermon-spouter's place, then help yourselves. Leave the bar here 'til last. Might as well enjoy the free drink! And one of you look to the horses. Get 'em corralled back of the livery.'

'What about McCreedy?'

'What about him?' grinned Knapp. 'If you see him, kill him.'

★　★　★

'Take about, oh, say an hour,' smiled Drayton from his seat at the table. He studied the bar clock for a moment. 'You want to start countin' down the last minutes of your town, Sheriff?'

Palmer stiffened, but stayed silent, his gaze still following the movements of Sol Gibbs' straining fingers.

A bar girl began to sniffle and whimper under Sheri Ward's protective arm.

'Shut that noise,' spat Drayton. 'Or mebbe she'd like me to shut it for her?'

The gang leader rose unsteadily to his feet, sweeping the whiskey bottle and glass to the floor, his eyes struggling to focus in the haze of smoke and liquor. The bar girl pressed closer to Sheri. Palmer's fists clenched. Boyd Knapp's back was still turned to the batwings where he stood on the boardwalk. This might be the moment, thought the sheriff, taking a step to place himself between Drayton and the girl.

It was then that Sol sprang upright from the chair, the ropes falling from him as he battled to squirm clear of the last of them. Drayton made to draw his Colt, but too late. Palmer's fist thudded into the leader's neck like a rock crashing him to the floor in a dazed heap.

'Get the girls out back and hide where you can,' ordered the sheriff, scrambling to grab Drayton's gun from its holster.

Sheri nodded and shepherded her flock away to the deeper shadows at the rear of the bar.

Palmer swung round to face the 'wings again where Sol had taken up position at the side of them and was motioning for the sheriff to draw Knapp's attention.

The gunslinger had already turned and was peering anxiously into the bar for a sight of Drayton when the sheriff kicked the bottle across the floor and waited, poised like a leopard, for Knapp to approach.

But it was the sudden stirring of Drayton and his groans as he struggled to find his feet that halted Knapp just short of the threshold. 'Frank — you all right in there?' he called.

Palmer winced and gestured for Sol to join him at the foot of the stairs. 'Get yourself clear of here,' he hissed. 'Go find Sheri and the girls and stay with 'em. No tellin' what them scumbags out there will do, but I can guess.'

He glanced quickly at Drayton still

struggling to stand, then at the 'wings where Knapp waited, his attention torn between the men in the street and the interior of the bar.

'What about you?' croaked Sol, his tired eyes bulging.

'Up there,' said Palmer, pointing to the balcony and rooms at the top of the stairs. 'Now get movin', f'crissake. Mebbe you'll find McCreedy. Mebbe Doc'll bring the men into town. Who knows? Just shift!'

Drayton had finally made it upright and was growling and spitting his way to the batwings when Sol disappeared through the back door and Sheriff Palmer to the darker reaches of the saloon bar's first-floor balcony.

★　★　★

Doc Walker led the town men on their return to Peppersville down the main trail in the full glare of the new morning light. He was close-flanked to his left and right by Byron Byam, Clyde

210

Harte, Ephraim Judd and Old Stoney. Behind him the jangle of tack, creak of leather, clip of hoofs and snorts of the mounts filled the air with their level tones at a steady, purposeful pace.

'I don't see this for bein' one of them occasions for sneakin' up on our town,' Doc had announced as they had prepared to ride out of cover. 'I reckon for us takin' this situation when the time comes by the scruff of its miserable neck. There'll be no standin' off, no backin' down. We ride in like we own the place — which we do, damn it!'

Now, as they came to within the last half-mile of the town, their gazes had tightened and narrowed, their hands tensed on what seemed to be suddenly heavy reins. They could smell the heat of the mounts against the freshness of the morning air, hear the sounds of their approach as if in some distant echo behind their thoughts.

Byam thought of his store, Sheriff Palmer, Sol and the mysterious Mr

McCreedy; Harte of Sheri, the girls and the state of his saloon; the undertaker of bodies and Boot Hill. Old Stoney's thoughts were of his business, the forge and stables, his worst fears reserved for his whispered prayers.

Doc Walker had decided hours ago that he was getting far too old for this sort of thing and that, if he did survive and live to see the return of Peppersville to the townsfolk, he would probably retire. But not before he had finally got to having a long talk with McCreedy who, now he came to think of it . . .

But that was as far as Doc's thoughts went. At the next turn in the trail, he could see the first lick of flame above the rooftops of the town and smell the drift of smoke.

22

Sheriff Palmer had opened the first door he had reached once into the shadowy, unlit balcony above the bar. The room, overlooking the street, had once been Clyde Harte's personal quarters with a trapdoor to a flight of rickety stairs that led directly to an alley-way flanking the saloon. Harte, like many a careful saloon-keeper, had planned his hurried escape priorities with care, thought the sheriff, positioning himself at the window.

He grunted, took a firmer grip on the Colt he had taken, and concentrated on the sounds around him: voices from the street below, the bellows of Drayton, clatter of boots on the boardwalks, banging of doors, smashing of glass, snorting and whinnying of horses. The gang were readying for their destruction of the town before riding on to their next conquest.

'Hell,' he hissed through clenched teeth, conscious for a moment of the throb in his hand. He closed his eyes, the images conjured in his thoughts swirling like a storm: Knapp's reference to North Rocks . . . the identity of what might be M.S . . . McCreedy . . . 'Damnit, where is the fella?' he hissed again, and tensed at the sudden shouts from the street.

'Find that sonofabitch lawman,' screamed Drayton. 'Kill him! Then go find them girls, you hear me? Find 'em, keep 'em, they're all yours!' The man thudded like a fevered bull from the boardwalk to the street. 'And I don't want to see no more of this town. Torch it!'

Palmer swallowed, began to sweat, but risked a quick glance over the scene below him. The gunslingers were working themselves to a frenzy of looting and destruction wherever they could. He wiped the sweat from his eyes. Would Sol, Sheri and the girls stay hidden or make a run for it? But to where?

More shouting, smashing, destruction. 'Go flush out them upstairs rooms in the bar,' called Knapp. 'Chances are the lawman's holed up in one of 'em.'

Palmer left the window, stared at the door, heard the thud of men making their way to the balcony, then felt his sweat freeze as he turned and watched the trapdoor inching open.

★　★　★

The sheriff trained his Colt on the trapdoor as it continued to lift like something taking slow breaths. Another half-inch, a pause, another breath higher, but still no sight of a hand.

He wiped the sweat hurriedly from his face, aware now of the quickening steps of the approaching sidekicks from the saloon below him. He glanced at the door as if hoping to see through it, then at the trapdoor inching on, sniffed and took two fast steps back to the window.

'Sons-of-goddamn-bitches!' he muttered as he watched the smoke cloud in shrouds from the direction of Preacher Peabody's place. He grunted at the sight of a licking tongue of flame, backed from the window and had half turned to watch the trapdoor again when the suddenly looming shadow of McCreedy reached across the room.

The man put a finger to his lips for silence and nodded towards the door to the balcony. The two men crept to it, McCreedy to the left, Palmer to the right.

'How many?' frowned the sheriff, listening to the sidekicks' subdued voices as they decided on the rooms to search.

McCreedy held up three fingers.

'We takin' them on?' hissed Palmer.

'Cover me,' said the man, drawing a Colt from its holster.

The sheriff tensed, sweated, watched McCreedy's free hand reach for the doorknob, tighten on it, then in one lightning movement, swing the door open. McCreedy was into the corridor, his gun blazing, almost before Palmer had swung himself away from the wall.

The Colt blazed in McCreedy's hand, throwing the sidekick nearest the open door back down the corridor as if whipped from his feet in a twister. A second gunslinger was already falling under the momentum of his dead partner when McCreedy's levelled blaze ripped into his chest then swung immediately to the right to take out the third man even as he blinked on the consuming stare of the shadowy shape about to kill him.

'Back to the room,' ordered McCreedy without a second glance at the bodies littering the balcony. 'Through the trap-door. Work your way up the street. Doc Walker's ridin' in with the town men.'

'Then what, f'crissake?' croaked Palmer. 'And what about you, mister? Ain't it about time — '

'Only time we've got, Sheriff, is for

savin' this town. And it's runnin' out fast, so shift!'

McCreedy bundled Palmer into the room and towards the trapdoor only seconds before the first explosion shook the town to its foundations.

★   ★   ★

The group of townsmen led by Doc Walker reined to a slithering dust-filled halt at the roar and crack of the explosion. Mounts bucked, pranced and snorted. Riders fought to calm and control their horses. The dirt swirled, the sunlight glared.

'What in the name of hell's goin' on in there?' shouted Harte above the sudden mayhem.

'Dynamite!' yelled a rider still struggling to stay in the saddle.

'They've found that supply of mine back of the store,' called Byam.

'Hold it, easy now,' urged Doc raising an arm as he reined his horse round to face the main party. 'Easy fellas, let's just reckon on the situation.'

'Ain't no reckonin' necessary, Doc,' said a man soothing his mount's neck. 'I figure for us all knowin' what Drayton's boys are doin' out there. They're torchin' and blastin' our town to oblivion.'

'Over my dead body they are!' growled Byam. 'If Peppersville's hittin' the dirt, I'm goin' with it, damnit.'

'All right, all right,' counselled Doc. 'So we ain't givin' in. 'Course we ain't, but we ain't ridin' to certain death neither.' He snapped the reins through his fingers. 'We break to two groups. Byam here will ride to the left, myself to the right. We keep clear of the main street 'til we've assessed the damage and the strength of Drayton's men. Shoot any of the scum on sight. We join up again at Old Stoney's forge.' Doc snapped the reins again. 'Split up and ride.'

A second explosion shuddered through the ground as the riders pulled away.

* * *

Palmer wiped the sweat-caked dirt and grime from his face and neck, steadied the aim of the Colt held firmly in his right hand, sensed the pressure on the trigger, and fired. The gunslinger silhouetted in the haze of smoke, dust and flames only yards from him fell face-down without a sound escaping his lips.

The sheriff grunted his satisfaction, blinked and slid quickly on to the next patch of shadow at the rear of Ephraim Judd's funeral parlour.

Another rat in Drayton's pack dead; one more step towards regaining the town. But, hell, he thought through another grunt as he smeared more dirt into the sweat on his face, there was a long way to go at this rate, always assuming he stayed lucky. He pressed himself deeper into the shadow cover as a string of explosions ripped through the smoke and heat-thickened air. The gunslingers had found the dynamite stored at the mercantile and were making the most of it. That, added to the fire they had started but which, thankfully, was still contained at the preacher's home, was satisfying the gang's appetite for now — but for how long, he wondered? Only a matter of time, surely, before they added to the fire and torched whatever they saw standing.

Palmer freshened his grip on the Colt and eased carefully from the shadow for a broader view of the street. No sign of Drayton or Knapp, nothing of McCreedy, and just where had Sheri, Sol and the girls holed up? He swung his gaze to left and right: scatterings of gunslingers, some looting and pillaging alone, like the one he had just shot, others working in packs of three and four.

He backed again, this time concentrating on the saloon. Drayton and Knapp had to be in there. McCreedy's shooting of the sidekicks on the balcony must have . . . He shrank instinctively into shade at the beat of hoofs, the sight of a group of townsmen riding in led by Doc Walker, guns already blazing, scattering the gunslingers to the cover of the buildings.

'Keep goin'. Take the livery,' shouted Doc as he urged the others on and reined to a halt just short of Palmer. 'Hell,' he gasped, sliding clumsily from the saddle, 'I was beginnin' to wonder if you were still alive.' He fell back into the shade. 'Sol and Sheri still breathin'? What about McCreedy?' He took a deep breath. 'Never mind. I've got Byam and the others circlin' in on the left there. If we get together . . . '

'We need to get to Drayton and Knapp,' said Palmer, his gaze scanning the street again.

'Not so easy from where I'm seein' things right now,' croaked Doc, cringing and ducking at the high and wide shots of the pillaging gunslingers.

'McCreedy's close, mebbe in the saloon. He's goin' to need help.' Palmer watched the street through narrowed eyes. 'I'm goin' to cross. Cover me best you can, then join up again with the others. Find Sol and Sheri. Get the girls safe.'

Another surge of explosions shattered the morning. Smoke curled and swirled. Dust and dirt clouded the air and light like a drifting mist.

'Go!' ordered Doc, slapping the sheriff's back as he drew his Colt in a fierce grip.

★   ★   ★

'See that? Did you see that?' spat Drayton, pushing an empty bottle to the floor. He stepped back from the saloon bar window. 'A whole bunch of them town scum ridin' in.' He growled and kicked a chair from his path as he crossed to the side of the batwings. 'Who in hell do they think they are? This is my town, damn it. Mine!' He swung round to face Boyd Knapp. 'Round up the boys. Let's go show them town men who's boss round here.'

'Too late,' said Knapp, cradling his shattered hand across him where he stood in the shadows at the bar.

'What do you mean too late?' snarled Drayton. 'What sorta talk is that?'

'Honest talk right now.' Knapp leaned back on the bar. 'This fella McCreedy is gettin' the better of you. You've got three bodies upstairs to prove that. And where is he now? You have any notion?'

Drayton spat. 'Who cares? The boys'll take care of him.'

'Better take a closer look at the boys out there. T'ain't so good for them neither, not now them townsmen are here. How long you figurin' before they group up and spit the lead like there's goin' to be no tomorrow? What price the boys then, all liquored up and girl-crazy like they are?'

The nerve in Drayton's cheek began to twitch. His glazed, glassy stare grew wetter and tighter. His fingers flexed at his side. 'So what you sayin' here, Boyd?' he mouthed as if summoning the words from some dark place.

'I'm sayin' as how you should mebbe rethink this situation. It's out of hand, Frank. This ain't another Leverton. Nothin' like it.' Knapp pushed himself clear of the bar and stood his ground without moving. 'Where's the woman and them girls? Where's the sheriff, his deputy? They're all out there, Frank, and it don't matter a damn how much you torch this town, the minute you step through them 'wings, you're a dead man.'

Drayton's lips broke to a sneering, cynical grin. 'Know somethin', Boyd, I could kill you soon as look at you. Never did rate you, anyhow.' He crossed the room slowly, his gaze fixed like a rattler's stare on Knapp's face, reached a table in the shadowed corner and lifted a Winchester from a mess of bottles and broken glasses. 'One of the boys got careless, eh?' he smiled. 'Left one of his pieces behind.' He rested the rifle across his shoulder. 'I could get to doin' a lot of damage with this. Don't have to tell you that, do I?'

'You could and mebbe you will, but I'm still tellin' you, Frank — '

Boyd Knapp did not get to telling anybody anything ever again. Midway through his next breath he was dead, shot clean through his neck — but not from the blaze of a Winchester.

23

Drayton plunged back to the shadows, his stare dazed but fixed like light on the sprawled, bleeding body of Knapp. He tightened his grip on the rifle, licked his lips and eased just far enough forward to let his gaze probe the balcony above the bar. Somebody up there. Had to be. No need for wild guesses. He could sense the presence like a nagging pain.

'That's got to be you, McCreedy,' he called. 'Still keepin' busy, I see. Well, you've kinda done me a favour. Was about to shoot that moanin' scumbag, anyhow. He weren't fit for the likes of the company of you and me.'

A crashing, shattering sound of breaking glass ripped across Drayton's voice. Men in the street whooped and yelled. A volley of shots set horses whinnying and snorting. A door crashed against an onslaught of bodies. An explosion added to the blistering mayhem.

'My boys are sure as hell havin' a time out there,' scoffed Drayton. 'Don't figure for it bein' long now before they're all through and what's left of this town ain't worth the pickin' over. What you reckon, McCreedy? We witnessin' the last of Peppersville? I figure so. And if anybody thinks them mad-head townsmen are goin' to make one jot of difference, they can think again. My boys'll see to that. You just watch. Meantime . . . '

Drayton had eased slowly through the shadows, edging ever closer to the bar and the one angle of vision that might give him a view of his target above him.

'Yeah, like I say, meantime we've got matters to talk over, eh? We can leave the others to the high jinks and hoedown, let's you and me get to some serious discussions.'

He was within a few steps of the

bar, the Winchester levelled at the hip, his gaze as watchful as a circling hawk's, the movements slow, careful, silent.

'Way I see it,' he went on, 'we got a lot in common. Reckon it: we work independent, using only what we need when we need it, and I figure for us both enjoyin' some of the finer things in life — good whiskey, classy women. And, my friend, here's the real point: we both know how to use a loaded piece, eh? How to make it the whole good reason for survival. Now that . . . '

His words faded at the sudden creak of the batwings behind him. He swung round, the rifle tensed. 'Who's there?' he croaked to nothing save the shadowy space and the softly swinging 'wing. 'Best show yourself, mister, whoever you are. I heard you sneak in, but I ain't in no mood . . . '

His words faded again at the squeak of a floorboard on the balcony. He turned, sweating now, his gaze narrowed and concentrated.

'Seems like we might have company, McCreedy.'

'You bet you have!' snarled Sheriff Palmer from the deepest shadows at the side of the batwings he had just reached.

Drayton's Winchester blazed ahead of tittering laughter. 'Well, if it ain't the lawman crept in here real quiet. And still breathin' and standin' I see. Hell, I should've done with you hours back!'

The Winchester blazed again, this time shattering the bar window, another roar splintering timbers.

'How long do you want for me to keep you alive, Sheriff?' spat Drayton. 'Just say the word, but I'm fast losin' patience here and I got other company to keep.'

A voice called from the street. 'Hey, Frank, get yourself out here, will yuh? We've been takin' this store apart plank by plank, and there's a whole heap of stuff waitin' for the pickin' over. Come and help yourself before these buzzards swallow the lot!'

A round of loose shots spat and crackled. Somewhere another window shattered. Voices lifted, broke into laughter then died behind the snorting of excited mounts.

Drayton flexed the rifle. 'You hear that, Sheriff? Hear that, McCreedy? The boys are wrappin' this up. We're about all through. Only a matter now of finishin' the torchin' . . . Stand aside there, Sheriff, if you give a tin-can for your life.'

Palmer's answer was to step from the shadows, his Colt drawn and levelled, the first blaze scorching over Drayton's shoulder like a surge of flame.

The Winchester roared, the shot searing the sheriff's left thigh. Palmer fell back with a groan, his leg bleeding, his shoulder throbbing, his gaze already beginning to swim and then cloud as he focused on the barrel of the rifle, the aim measured and steady.

Drayton grinned, his lips wet, the nerve behind the scar twitching with excitement.

A floorboard creaked somewhere in the darker depths of the balcony.

The shouting in the street reached a new climax. Another window shattered. Another door collapsed.

'Torch the place! Put it to the flame!' screamed a voice hysterically.

'See what I mean, Sheriff?' sneered Drayton. 'Looks like the end of the line — and that goes for you too, mister.'

The gang leader had eased through a slow step when the mayhem in the street erupted to a new level at the sound of pounding hoofs approaching from the far end of the street.

Doc Walker and the townsmen, thought Palmer, taking the seconds of Drayton's broken concentration to squirm best he could back to the shadows at the side of the 'wings.

'What the hell,' blustered Drayton, swinging the rifle clear of its aim on the sheriff as he moved to scan the street.

Shots, shouts, snorts filled the dust-swirling air. Palmer heard Doc yelling his orders to 'get among 'em, boys,' winced at the sudden non-stop blaze and roar of gunfire, more shattering glass, more crashing timbers as the very body and soul of the town seemed to creak, groan and splinter under the onslaught.

Drayton scanned the scene from the 'wings as if taking in the sights of the very fires of hell itself, then, shaken back to the reality behind him, swung round, the Winchester blazing blindly into the gloom.

'On your feet, lawman, wherever you're skulkin',' he growled, advancing deeper into the bar. 'I said — '

'He heard you.'

The voice came out of the shadows on the stairs to the balcony, an assured, confident, commanding voice that seemed apart from the hellfire in the street.

'McCreedy?' croaked Drayton. 'You're still here.' He swallowed and wiped the sweat from his face. 'Just who the devil are you, mister? I ain't never crossed you before, ain't never kept your company. So what's the deal? You cuttin' yourself in on my outfit? You want a part of it?'

Drayton's gaze narrowed as he probed the shadows. 'Why don't you step out here, let me get a good look at you?'

Palmer lay perfectly still in the darkness at the wall, his head reeling with the chaos in the street, the drone of Drayton's voice, a tension in the bar that heightened the slightest creak to an echoing crash.

The barrel of the Winchester glinted as Drayton eased it forward. 'Suit yourself, mister, but I ain't got no more time for messin . . . '

The rifle spat viciously through a booming roar that threatened to burst the bar at its seams. But it was as the echo faded and the street sounds filled the bar again that a Colt blazed from the balcony. Four fast shots that tossed Drayton back to a flotsam of chairs, tables, smashed bottles and glasses and left him for dead, a tangle of limbs, staring eyes and blood in the debris of his own making.

It was a full minute before a dust-coated Doc Walker burst through the batwings and stood gasping on the edge of the gloom. 'You there, Sheriff?' he gulped. 'Thought you should be the first to know as how Sheri, Sol and the girls are safe at the livery. And don't you fret none, we've got them gunslingin' scumbags under control. No doubtin' to that!' He stepped deeper into the bar to within a few feet of the body of Frank Drayton. 'Well, now, ain't that some welcome sight? I'd say we've won back our town, wouldn't you?'

24

Byron Byam strolled casually through the early-evening shadows, his gaze gentle, a glow of satisfaction lighting up his face, his pace easy and relaxed as he reached the end of the boardwalk, took the lapels of his frock-coat in firm hands and heaved a sigh of relief.

It was all going to plan, coming together almost without a hitch or hindrance. Another couple of weeks and his new store would be open for business as usual, the Broken Nugget fully refurbished and decorated, the damaged buildings repaired and functional again, and Preacher Peabody installed in a rebuilt home with the affable Hetty Stone employed as his housekeeper. No doubt about it, he thought, Peppersville had survived the Drayton gang's attack, was back on the map and all set to prosper.

But there was just one snag; the snag that had always seemed to be there. Where was McCreedy?

Byam grunted, relaxed his grip on the lapels and turned to greet Sheriff Palmer and Sol Gibbs approaching on their early-evening town rounds.

'All quiet, Sheriff,' smiled the store-keeper.

'Like you say, Byron, all quiet,' said Palmer, welcoming the chance to rest his leg.

The three men were silent for a moment as their gazes roved over the settled town, peaceful in the glow of the first lanterns trimmed and lit in quiet windows.

'Any news?' asked Byam carefully.

'About McCreedy? Nothin'.' Palmer eased his Winchester to his side. 'Leastways, nothin' we ain't already certain of. No question in my mind, though, he's headed somewhere to join up with M.S. — Matt Stewart — Marshall Matt Stewart as I've now been able to confirm for a fact. My guess would be they're in North Rocks or thereabouts.'

'He was no school teacher, that's for sure!' said Byam. 'But was he a lawman?'

'No record of him bein' so,' murmured Sol. 'We've checked. And Marshal Stewart retired some while back.'

'So where does that leave us?' frowned Byam.

Palmer cradled the Winchester and stared into the fast-approaching darkness. 'It leaves us where it's always seemed to leave us — with a fella, name of McCreedy, who came to us as teacher for the school. Rode in, recommended and vouched for, from back east — and then, would you believe, set about helpin' us beat the Drayton threat. And did it almost single-handed, damn it! If it hadn't been for him . . . well, I guess that don't need no spellin' out, does it?'

'And then disappears before the dust had time to finger a fella's throat,' added Sol. 'Just vanished without a word. But, hell, we sure won the town again! Them gunslingers of Drayton's who weren't already destined for a pine box rode like the wind once they knew Drayton and Boyd were dead and we got to settin' about 'em.'

'Say that again,' agreed Byam. He sighed. 'Losses, pain, but we're still here and should be grateful for that.' His gaze moved slowly over the street. 'Even so, there's still the problem of McCreedy, who he really was, where he hailed from, why he was trailin' the Drayton gang like he did, and where, darn it, he disappeared to. Know somethin', I don't figure for us settin' eyes on the fella again . . . '

Nor did they, and the events of those days, the personal exploits and experiences of men and women alike were to pass slowly, not to say, colourfully, into the annals of Peppersville's history.

Leastways, they did until the arrival in town one fine summer's day of Herbert D. Harrington.

Harrington, a much respected and renowned scribe for the famous *Eastern Daily Tribune*, was in the process of completing a series of articles on the growth and development of the newly opened and populated West and the people involved.

'And believe me, gentlemen, I am talking about *all* men, the good as well as the bad,' he had told a gathering of the town elders in the saloon bar of the Broken Nugget. 'You've had your share of both, I know,' he had added quietly. 'I refer, of course, to the Drayton gang and the death in this very town — this very bar — of the notorious Frank Drayton.'

'Darn near the very spot where you're standin', mister,' Ephraim Judd had offered with an adjustment of his pince-nez and much to the amusement of the others — Sheriff Palmer, Sol Gibbs, Byron Byam, Clyde Harte, Doc Walker, Preacher Peabody, Old Stoney, Sheri and the girls — surrounding him. 'Know that for a fact. Laid him out fittin' for the Good Lord he still had a right to see with my own hands.'

'The very stuff of history,' Harrington had enthused on a flurry of his fingers. 'And his killer, what of him?'

The gathering had remained silent.

'Well, there is something to be told, as I have discovered,' Harrington went on. 'Did you know, for example, that the man who finally put an end to the Draytons' rule of terror over so many years had witnessed the death of his own sister at the hands of Charlie Drayton, his brothers, Morgan Reights and Boyd Knapp while visiting her at the school where she was a teacher out Kansas way? Did you know that?'

'That would explain how it was . . . ' began Preacher Peabody, only to hear his voice fade on a sudden swallow.

'Mebbe it was her we should have had as our teacher here,' murmured Byam. 'Mebbe he took her place.'

'Well, I'll be damned,' added Doc.

Harrington cleared his throat and continued: 'It was this heinous crime and violation that drove the man to join forces with a certain Marshal Stewart in pursuit of the murderers. But, there again, perhaps you knew all of this. I have merely recorded the details as I have discovered them. And yet there remains a gap, and that, of course, is the man himself and what happened, *really* happened, here in Peppersville. There, dare I say it, lies the enigma and the intrigue. So what can you tell me of the man who was only ever known as McCreedy? Where, I wonder, do we begin?'

THE END

We do hope that you have enjoyed reading this large print book.

Did you know that all of our titles are available for purchase?

We publish a wide range of high quality large print books including:
Romances, Mysteries, Classics
General Fiction
Non Fiction and Westerns

Special interest titles available in large print are:
The Little Oxford Dictionary
Music Book, Song Book
Hymn Book, Service Book

Also available from us courtesy of Oxford University Press:
Young Readers' Dictionary
(large print edition)
Young Readers' Thesaurus
(large print edition)

For further information or a free brochure, please contact us at:
Ulverscroft Large Print Books Ltd.,
The Green, Bradgate Road, Anstey,
Leicester, LE7 7FU, England.
Tel: (00 44) 0116 236 4325
Fax: (00 44) 0116 234 0205

Whilst on military patrol for the United States Cavalry, Lieutenant Raoul Webster is blinded in a freak accident. Guided by his young brother, he sets out for San Francisco to consult an eye doctor. But, en route, their stagecoach is ambushed by ruthless Mexican bandits. Raoul's brother is murdered, as are the driver and all the male passengers. Raoul survives, but he is alone in the wilderness and vulnerable to all Fate can throw at him. He is kept alive by one burning ambition, to track down his brother's killer . . .

SIX-SHOOTER JUNCTION

David Bingley

Deputy Sheriff Sam Regan considered he had been lucky when he found an outlaw's horseshoe mark outside the Bankers Hotel in Blackwood after a bank raid. He overtook a raider and was badly shaken to learn that the outlaw was Pete Arnott, a boyhood friend. The meeting, however, led to gun play and Sam had to kill Pete. He tried to hide the fact that Pete was an outlaw, but the truth leaked out to certain important people who insisted on Sam chasing the raiders and proving the link between Pete and the gang . . .

FLINT'S BOUNTY

Ben Coady

The town of Eagle Junction has two headaches — the prolonged drought and the threat of revenge from the Galt gang. Having killed Ben Galt, brother of the notorious Jack Galt, the marshal has fled town. His deputy, every bit as alert to the danger, has followed his example. Meanwhile, Dan Straker, a drought-stricken farmer, is loading up his last supplies from Arthur Flint's store. Without supplies he's done for and Flint can no longer extend credit to him. Then, a dangerous option is revealed to Straker . . .

LOBO AND HAWK

Jake Douglas

One was a Yankee. One was a Rebel. They were the only two survivors of the bombardment of a New Mexico town at the end of the Civil War. After trying unsuccessfully to kill each other, they decided to become partners and go after some Confederate gold that was up for grabs. The trouble was that they weren't the only ones who knew about the hoard. Soon there would be trouble enough to bring back old hostilites, and only blazing guns would settle the matter. But who would live?

HONDO COUNTY GUNDOWN

Chad Hammer

The Valley of the Wolf was no place for strangers, but Chet Beautel was not the usual breed of drifter. He was a straight-shooting man of the mountains searching for something better than what lay behind. Instead, he encountered a new brand of terror enshrouded in a mystery which held a thousand people hostage — until he saddled up to challenge it with a mountain man's grit and courage, backed up by a blazing .45. If Wolf Valley was ever to be peaceful again, Chet Beautel would be that peacemaker.